(

*Ghost Island* is the fif .
The other titles in the e
*Up, It's Midnight!;* d
*Locked Doors* and *Dead Man's Chest.*
This book is complete in itself, but the plot follows on from the non-Naitabal story *Skeletons in the Attic.*

NAITABAL: A wild species of human, aged about ten, a cross between a native and a cannibal.

NAITABAL LANGUAGE: Language used by Naitabals to confuse enemies and adults.

NAITABAL TREE: Any large tree (preferably oak) suitable for habitation by Naitabals.

NAITABAL SEAS AND: ISLANDS Areas of land occupied by Naitabals and/or their enemies.

NAITABAL TERRITORY: Territory controlled by Naitabals – marked as 'N.T.' on most maps.

*David Schutte was born in Crouch End, North London. Brain surgeon, pop singer and Olympic athlete are just some of the things he never achieved. Apart from being an author, he is also a specialist children's bookseller. He lives in Hampshire with his wife and children.*

*Also by David Schutte*

SAM and the U.F.O.

*The Naitabal Mystery series:*

1. DANGER, KEEP OUT!
   (Originally published as MUD PIES AND WATER-BOMBS)

2. WAKE UP, IT'S MIDNIGHT!

3. WILD WOODS, DARK SECRET

4. BEHIND LOCKED DOORS

SKELETONS IN THE ATTIC (A non-Naitabal *prequel* to GHOST ISLAND)

5. GHOST ISLAND

6. DEAD MAN'S CHEST

Non-fiction:

WILLIAM – THE IMMORTAL An illustrated Bibliography

DAVID SCHUTTE

# GHOST ISLAND

A Naitabal Mystery

To Nicola

Best wishes

David Schutte

Junior Genius

First published in 2001 by Junior Genius
93 Milford Hill, Salisbury, Wiltshire SP1 2QL

ISBN 1-904028-05-5



1 3 5 7 9 8 6 4 2

A CIP catalogue record for this book is available from the British Library

Printed in the U.K. by
Polestar AUP Aberdeen Ltd

TO

NIGEL

WITH LOVE

## *Rules for Speaking Naitabal Language*

Words beginning with A: Add 'ang' to the end.
e.g. apple = *apple-ang*. The word 'a', however, is just *ang*.

Words beginning with B,C or D: move the first letter to the end of the word, then add 'ang' to the end.
e.g. banana = *anana-bang*; catapult = *atapult-cang*;
disaster = *isaster-dang*.

Words beginning with E: Add 'eng' to the end.
e.g. elephant = *elephant-eng*.

Words beginning with F,G or H: move the first letter to the end of the word, then add 'eng' to the end.
e.g. fool = *ool-feng*; groan = *roan-geng*; help = *elp-heng*.

Words beginning with I: Add 'ing' to the end.
e.g. ink = *ink-ing*. The word 'I', however, is just *Ing*.

Words beginning with J,K,L,M, or N: move the first letter to the end of the word, then add 'ing' to the end.
e.g. jump = *ump-jing*; kill = *ill-king*; laugh = *augh-ling*;
measles = *easles-ming*; night = *ight-ning*.

Words beginning with O: Add 'ong' to the end.
e.g. orange = *orange-ong*.

Words beginning with P,Q,R,S, or T: move the first letter to the end of the word, then add 'ong' to the end.
e.g. parrot = *arrot-pong*; queen = *een-quong* (notice that 'qu' stays together); rabbit = *abbit-rong*;
sausage = *ausage-song*; tickle = *ickle-tong*.

Words beginning with U: Add 'ung' to the end.
e.g. under = *under-ung*.

Words beginning with V,W,X,Y or Z: Move the first letter to the end of the word, then add 'ung' to the end.
e.g. vest = *est-vung*; witch = *itch-wung*; xylophone = *ylophone-xung*; young = *oung-yung*; zebra = *ebra-zung*.

For words beginning with CH,GH,PH,RH,SH,TH, or WH, move the 'H' with the first letter, but follow the 'first letter' rules.
e.g. chop = *op-chang*; ghost = *ost-gheng*; photo = *oto-phong*;
rhesus = *esus-rhong*; shop = *op-shong*;
thistle = *istle-thong*; why = *y-whung*.

For plurals, keep the 's' in the original position.
e.g. book = *ook-bang*; books = *ooks-bang*;
pig = *ig-pong*; pigs = *igs-pong*.

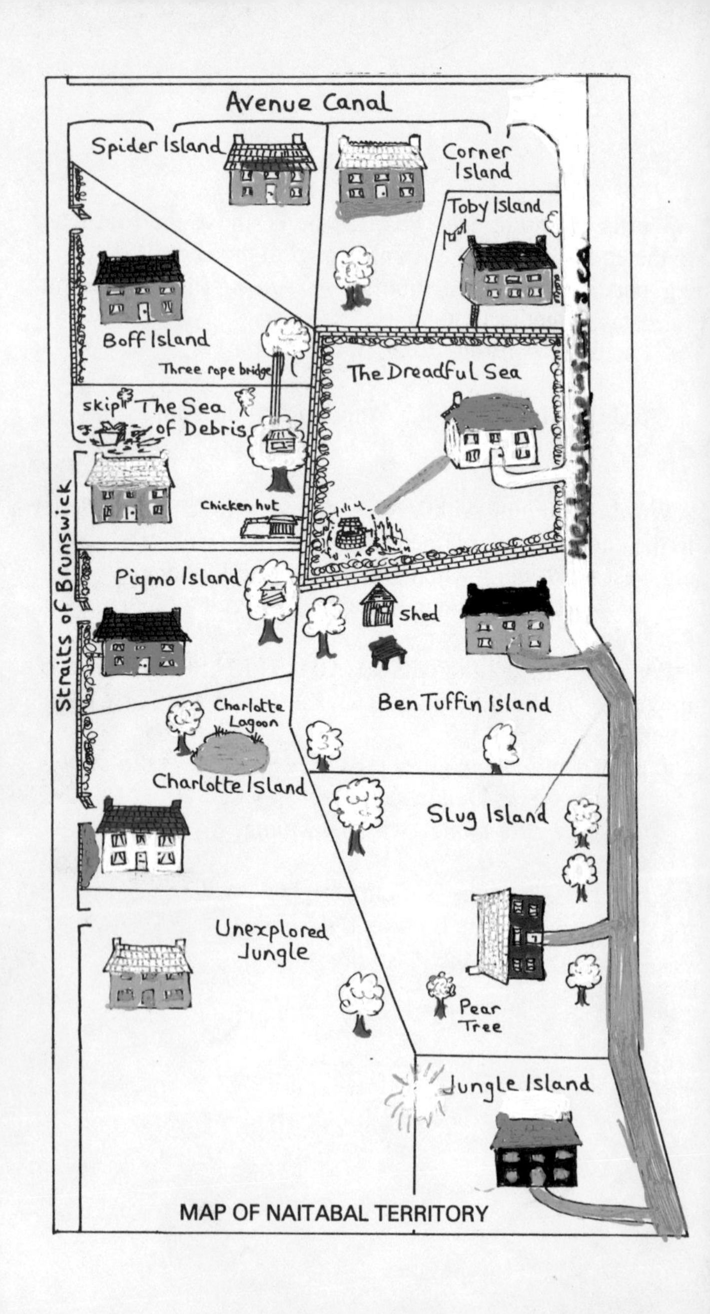


MAP OF NAITABAL TERRITORY

*Contents*

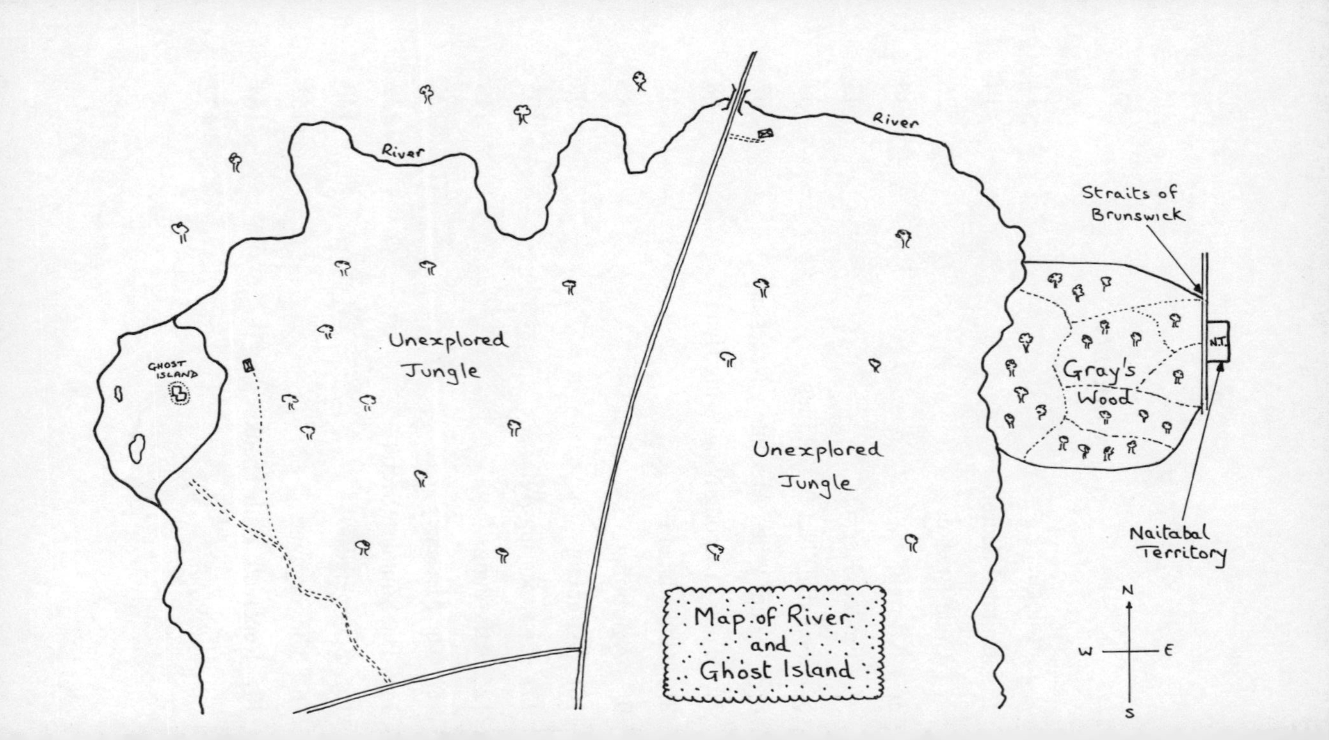
River
River
GHOST ISLAND
Unexplored Jungle
Unexplored Jungle
Straits of Brunswick
Gray's Wood
N.T.
Naitabal Territory
Map of River and Ghost Island
N
W
E
S

## PROLOGUE

The stranger emerges from the railway station. He is about thirteen years old with dark hair and his face is serious and full of purpose. It is already dark, and the quiet streets are glowing yellow from the light of the sodium lamps. He crosses to the road opposite and begins striding confidently, counting turnings as he goes. First right, second right, third right. He glances back over his shoulder for the hundredth time of his journey, making sure no one has followed him. As he takes the third turn to the right, he slips into the shadow of a front garden, then stands for several minutes, waiting. No one comes, no one follows. Now he hurries, crossing the road to take the first left. Every now and then he raises a hand to his coat pocket, pressing it gently, feeling if the envelope is still safe inside.

He follows the road round a curve to the left, passes a turning on the right, then veers left, and left again. He pauses on the corner, finally making sure that he is alone. The wind stirs the trees in the woods that loom opposite, and he feels a shiver of apprehension and excitement.

Now he is counting houses: the second on the left. In the pale yellow light he can see the skip filling its front garden, overflowing with builder's rubble. Nailed to a tree to his left is the notice, just as he has been told. It is barely legible in the half-light as the shadows of wind-blown branches dance on its message:

He breathes a sigh of relief.

He gives one last nervous glance over his shoulder then plunges across the pile of bricks and rubble that blocks the pathway to the side of the house. Now he is in the garden behind the house and there is hardly any light at all. His feet pick their way through more piles of jumble, and he can see at last the massive silhouette of an oak tree in front of him, black against the sky. He can also make out, brooding in its branches, the dark and rectangular outline of a tree-house. A ghostly light glows within.

Remembering his instructions, he stands below it, then cups his hands, folding his thumbs together to make a whistle. He blows on them, adjusting his hands until the doleful moan of wasted air becomes the throaty whistle of an owl. Once, twice, three times he blows the signal.

Immediately there are clicks and creaks in the darkness above him. Something rattles and falls near his side, but doesn't hit the ground. Instead, it writhes and twitches in mid-air, and he reaches out a hand and steadies it. It is a rope ladder.

"Code-name?" says a whisper from above.

"Peter."

"Password?"

"Naitabal secrets."

"Come up, Peter."

Peter, the young stranger, climbs the ladder carefully, feeling it sway and twist with each movement he makes. Someone switches on a torch and he finds four faces smiling down to greet him, and two pairs of arms pulling him inside. He stands upright on the sturdy floorboards as a pair of hands haul up the rope ladder behind him. More hands close the trap-door.

Four children introduce themselves in whispers – the Naitabals – Boff, Charlotte, Toby and Ben. They tell him that the fifth Naitabal, Jayne, is on holiday.

"Were you followed?" they ask.

"No."

Peter the Stranger reaches into his coat pocket and pulls out the precious envelope. He hands it to them.

"This is it," he says.

## CHAPTER ONE

# *Naitabal Secrets*

Charlotte reached a dense clump of trees in the middle of Gray's Wood and stopped running. The heavy coils of rope were biting into her shoulder. She shifted the weight to a more comfortable position, then held her breath and listened into the steady breeze. Light footsteps were padding in the distance, hurrying towards her. The rope was still hurting. She hoisted it on to the other shoulder and headed for an oak tree that stood a few metres off the track. Side-stepping behind the trunk, she strained forward until she could just see along the path the way she had come. The sound of her own breathing filled her ears. For a moment she could hear nothing else. Had the footsteps stopped? She held her breath again and listened.

The footsteps didn't come.

She waited longer, nearly a minute perhaps, still holding her breath. Still no one came. At last the air exploded from her lungs. Panting noisily, she moved back to the path, ears straining. This time she heard the crack of a twig in the middle distance, then the crisp rustle of dead leaves, a branch swishing through the air.

She stopped again, dodged behind another tree, waited two more minutes.

At last she heard the footsteps again, pounding on the dusty track, breaking into a trot. As they approached she pressed herself against the bark, hiding, not daring to look in case she was seen. When the footsteps had thudded past the tree, she inched her way round the trunk, trying to catch a glimpse of her pursuer.

The footsteps stopped. Charlotte moved back instinctively, out of sight, waiting. The enemy moved on.

Creeping back round the tree with one cautious eye, she saw him at last, the tallish, slim figure in shadow. He had stopped again, further along the winding dirt track between the trees. His head was hidden by branches, so all she could see was his jumper, but that was enough to recognise him. The figure moved again, and she caught a glimpse of the back of his head as he moved off. He was twisting this way and that, listening, watching, trying to find her.

As soon as he was out of range, Charlotte doubled back. She ran at a tangent towards the far north-western edge of the wood, breaking into a Naitabal chant as she went.

"*Naitabals can do anything*," she sang, congratulating herself. "*Naitabals can go anywhere*."

She wondered how Toby was getting on.

Three hundred metres away, Toby, too, was trying to shake off a pursuer. He was lying flat on his stomach, keeping as still as he could. Next to him, tucked behind a tangle of dead brambles, was a big white plastic drum. The grass and dry leaves all around him stirred as the moving air hurried through the wood. He pressed his ear to the ground, waiting for the hiss to die down. Soon a lull came, the breeze dropped, and for a few seconds there was perfect silence. He wondered if Charlotte had been successful. Almost immediately he heard – then felt – the rhythmic pounding of feet not many trees away. He froze until the danger had passed. When the sound had receded and he was sure it was safe, he stood up, slung the plastic drum on to his back, then cut away from the direction of the footsteps at an angle of a hundred and thirty-five degrees.

He ran, barefoot, heading like a magnet towards the same Naitabal secret that was pulling Charlotte with the same powerful force.

He wondered how Ben was doing.

Ben Tuffin, the third Naitabal, sat on the low front wall of his house, dangling his legs over the pavement, waiting. Next to him, propped against the wall, was a long plank of wood. The pair of them waited patiently, the plank silent, Ben humming a tune. Soon, as Ben had expected, a figure appeared at the distant corner of Meadow Lane (known to the Naitabals as the Meadow Lane-ian Sea). The figure, believing itself to be not only invisible, but clever and cunning, dived into a nearby front garden. Ben watched as he recognised Cedric Morgan, the leader of the enemy Igmopong. He was making his way towards Ben, trying to stalk him, climbing from garden to garden, making pathetic attempts to keep himself out of sight. But the violent rocking of bushes, trees and shrubs along his trajectory made his position no secret. He had as much chance of going unnoticed, thought Ben, as an elephant tiptoeing through a two-ton bag of crisps.

When the violent twitching reached a mature laurel hedge two gardens away, Ben saw a bald-headed elderly figure emerge from the front door of the house. It grabbed Cedric by the shoulders, squashed him into the hedge so he couldn't move, and started shouting at him. It was HMS *Slugface*, their half-mad neighbour who had once been Naitabal Enemy Number One*. Ben could hear his shrill screech and some of the words: 'trespassing', 'lesson', 'my garden' and 'pay for this'. Ben knew his opportunity had come. He slipped quietly from the wall, leaving the plank on guard, and ran along the side of his own house on to Ben Tuffin Island. (To ordinary people, of course, it was just Ben's garden.) He stood near the back fence and glanced up at his house. He wanted to make doubly sure that no one was

---

* See *Wake Up, It's Midnight!*

watching from the windows. His father was in the attic installing some new lights. His mother was decorating a front bedroom at the moment, pretending to be Elvis Presley. He could hear her specially-deepened voice through the open window, telling passers-by they could do anything, as long as they didn't step on her blue suede hues.

Ben glanced across at Pigmo Island, where Cedric Morgan and the enemy Igmopong had their headquarters. It was empty and silent, with no eyes spying down from its ramshackle tree-house. Andy and Doris, he knew, had followed Charlotte and Toby into the woods, while Cedric was being slowly shouted to death by HMS *Slugface*. He could see Amanda Wilson some distance away, at the entrance to the Sea of Debris, watching in vain for Jayne, the fourth Naitabal, hoping to follow her. But Ben knew she was already too late. Jayne had gone, and he knew exactly where she was.

The coast was clear. Ben ducked down behind the big garden shed and lay down flat amongst the weeds and grass. Slowly, he eased himself forward until his head and shoulders were underneath the shed. Stretching further, he used his fingers to brush away the dry earth until they found the solid wooden surface underneath. He finished scraping the earth away, feeling for the corners with his fingertips, then pushed a hand under the edge of the wooden board and lifted. He'd had plenty of practice. He raised the board easily and pushed it to one side, making sure that it stayed out of sight under the shed. He could already see the entrance to the Naitabal tunnel. He backed away, turned himself round so that he was lying on his stomach with his feet under the shed, then wriggled slowly backwards into the half-metre-wide square hole. He felt the cool air on his legs as he slithered backwards and down into the darkness.

Once inside and crouching down, Ben switched on his torch. He reached up and pulled the wooden cover back into place. As it fell into the recess with a dull little thud, Ben turned and shone his torch along the tunnel. The tunnel was another Naitabal secret. None of the Naitabals could remember how long it had taken them to build it. Mr Elliott, their builder friend, had shown them how to do it safely, and now inspected it regularly. Ben looked at the wooden planks of the floor that stretched further than his torchlight into darkness, and couldn't help admiring the sturdy uprights and the wood-lined walls and roof. It looked like a long, narrow box.

He crawled forward on his knees, four metres, five. He would be under the corner of the Dreadful Sea by now. A few metres further on, he stopped. He was at the entrance to the branch tunnel on his right. He waited, listening. He could already hear the scrambling, thudding noises up ahead. A few moments later, the beam of another torch flickered on the tunnel floor and walls. Then its source came into view, a bright light moving rhythmically up and down as the hand that held it crawled towards him from the opposite direction.

"Hi, Jayne!" he whispered.

"Hi, Ben!" said Jayne.

"All clear at my end."

"Mine, too. I got rid of the stupid Igmopong. Amanda's standing like a dope waiting for me to finish feeding the chickens."

"Cedric's been caught by HMS *Slugface*," said Ben. "He must be wondering if he's ever going to see his mother again."

They both giggled, their voices sounding spooky in the hollow space.

Ben turned right into the branch tunnel, and Jayne followed, full of excitement and anticipation. Only a few metres further on, they came to a tiny square wooden door with a padlock on it. Ben contorted himself to reach the key in his pocket, found it, and undid the lock. He opened the door. Jayne squeezed alongside, dying to see what the other Naitabals had hidden while she'd been on holiday.

They shone their torches into the black void. The two beams met in a blaze of light on the newest Naitabal secret.

Boff, the fifth Naitabal, was sitting in one corner of the Naitabal tree-house with a writing pad. There was a big frown on his forehead, and he was writing and scribbling and crossing things out. At regular intervals he stood up and checked the view through the three windows. Much as he wanted to solve the puzzle he was working on, it was vital that he kept watch for the enemy Igmopong.

To the north he could see Boff Island (his own garden next door), with its big oak tree and the three-rope bridge looping towards him. To the west lay the Sea of Debris, full of indispensable rubbish. To the south was the chicken hut, and behind that, the fence that separated them from their enemies on Pigmo Island. Further to the south lay Charlotte Island, with Ben Tuffin Island to the left. There was still no sign of the enemy, apart from Amanda. She was standing at the entrance to the Sea of Debris looking twice as useless as a spare tyre on a hovercraft.

Boff cleaned his glasses, double-checked that the red flag was handy near the south window, sat down again, and carried on scribbling. He took alternate glances out of the windows, then up at the newspaper cutting that was pinned to the wall in front of him. Every time he glanced at the cutting, the furrows etched more deeply into his brow.

He didn't know how long he'd been concentrating when the Naitabal bell beneath the tree-house suddenly cavorted as it was hit by a volley of acorns from below. He stood up and looked through the west window. Charlotte and Toby were back, anxious to come up. He opened the trap-door at his feet and rolled out the rope ladder. They climbed inside, and Toby closed the trap-door. They found hot drinks in the vacuum flasks in the cupboard under the branch.

Charlotte took a few welcome sips and laughed.

"Andy tried to follow me," she announced, "but it was easy enough to shake him off."

"It's pathetic," said Toby. "Doris tried the same with me, but she didn't have a clue."

"It's getting beyond a joke now," said Boff, seriously. "We can't do *anything* without finding the stupid Igmopong spying on us. We'll have to do something about it."

"It's only because they haven't got any minds of their own," said Charlotte. "Poor things. They can't think of anything to occupy their idle brains, so they follow us to see what we're doing."

"They've seen us taking ropes and planks and chairs and massive plastic containers into Gray's Wood," said Toby. "But they haven't seen where we've taken them. It won't be a secret much longer if they start guessing."

"The whole thing's taking too long, having to dodge them all the time," said Boff. "We'll never get it built at this rate."

Charlotte closed the west window against the draught and frowned at the strange newspaper cutting and Boff's scribbles.

"Haven't you solved it yet?" she said.

Boff shook his head, annoyed with himself. The puzzle that had appeared in the local newspaper was no Naitabal secret. It was there for the whole community to see – but Boff wanted to be the first to solve it.

Ben and Jayne's torches were pointing down into darkness. It was a room he and Jayne had reached – an underground room with a secret history*, used by the Naitabals for hiding very special secrets. Their torches had picked out a small metal box below them, resting on one of the benches that

---

* See *Danger, Keep Out!*

bounded the walls.

Jayne was the only Naitabal who hadn't seen the letter with its secret message inside. The strange thing had happened when she'd been away, staying with a cousin for a few days. A stranger had telephoned – a boy of thirteen – and arranged to come and see them in secret one evening. The Naitabals had discussed whether to wait for Jayne's return before seeing the stranger, but his need was urgent and they had decided not to delay. He had handed over an envelope for safe-keeping, and told them to read its contents. He wouldn't discuss anything, but disappeared back into the night to catch his train home. What the Naitabals had found inside the envelope was one of the most intriguing mysteries they had ever seen.

Now Jayne would be able to see it for the first time. The journey through the tunnel had been exciting enough – it always was – but the thought of visiting their secret room to look at a new Naitabal secret was almost more than she could bear.

"Ready?" said Ben.

Jayne needed no encouragement. She slithered down hands first through the tiny door and dropped on to the bench below. She stood up, then turned her torch for Ben to follow. They automatically brushed off their clothes as they approached the box in the gloom. Ben turned the key, and Jayne opened the lid. She saw the envelope lying inside, with the word 'NAITABALS' on it in capital letters. It was marked 'URGENT', with Ben's address and a stamp in case it was ever mislaid.

"Good. It's still safe," said Ben.

Jayne was so excited she could hardly grip the envelope.

"Shall I open it?"

Ben nodded eagerly in the torchlight.

With shaking hands, Jayne took out the letter and read it.

*Dear Naitabals,*

*My code-name is Peter and I am thirteen years old. You don't know me, but I was given your address by a friend who knows you and says that you help people to solve difficult problems. My friend says you can all be trusted to the end of the universe.*

*My problem is a simple one. All I need is for something to be hidden. I want you to hide it for me – and hide it so well that no one else will ever find it. In the enclosed envelope you will find an old letter and a message in code. Together, they could send someone to prison. Or – I suppose if they fall into the wrong hands – they could make a certain criminal very rich. This Bad Man is very powerful, and if I give these papers to the police, my life will be in danger – because he'll want revenge. But if they are kept together in secret, the fact that they exist will protect me from the Bad Man.*

*It's only fair that I tell you the story so that you understand how important it is for the secret to remain hidden. I inherited these papers from my mother, who hid them for the first thirteen years of my life. The Bad Man was her partner all those years ago, and when she discovered the letter – and what it meant – she ran away from him. The man who wrote it died the following day in police custody. No one else knows anything. My mother died recently and left these papers to me. But now the Bad Man has found me and I can't risk keeping them in my house. I don't want to destroy them, either, in case the Bad Man starts his old tricks again. As long as he knows the letter still exists, I know he'll behave himself. I thought if I sent them to you, you could find a really safe place for them. I don't need you (or anyone) to crack the code. I don't think it would help to know its secret.*

*I know this sounds morbid, but if ever I die in suspicious circumstances, then you have my permission to crack the code and reveal its contents and the letter to the police, or anyone you think appropriate. I shall tell the Bad Man that I have instructed those who hold the code to do this if anything happens to me. That way I should be safe.*

*Please don't contact me unless it's truly vital – in case I'm being watched. My phone could be tapped – who knows?*

*I am indebted to you forever,*

*Your very sincere friend, and friend-of-a-friend,*

*'Peter'.*

Jayne looked across at Ben in the torchlight.

"Ben!" she said. "It's scary! What does it mean?"

"Look in the other one," said Ben.

Slowly, Jayne extracted the other envelope. It was addressed to someone the Naitabals had never heard of, and the stamp and postmark were crisp and clear – and fourteen years old.

"I'm sure Peter meant we could *look* at it," said Ben. "He said we didn't *need* to crack the code, as long as we keep it safe."

Jayne pulled out the contents. First, there was a letter.

*Frank,*

*Here's your copy of the code showing where I've hidden the stuff. Keep it safe until it blows over. Someone may have welshed on me, so if I'm jugged, we'll have to square it when I get out. If they come for me, I'll burn my copy, so don't worry.*

*Reg.*

With the letter was a coded message. It was new to Jayne, of course, but Ben had seen it before. As he looked over her shoulder he wondered for the umpteenth time what it meant:

```
TNQBM HLVII ENQLF YUNEO SLVMQ RVKEG
TIVKG BBPOQ 24793 3TXGT YVVIZ SSHFX
```

Jayne was intrigued.

"Has Boff tried to break this code?"

"No," said Ben. "We decided not to try because of what Peter says in his letter. Anyway, Boff's still working on that other strange advert in the newspaper."

Jayne looked at the letter and the code a little longer, then carefully replaced both sheets in the small envelope and put everything back in the box.

"Come on," said Ben. "We'd better go now and see how the others have done."

They climbed out through the door in the wall above the bench, padlocked it again, and crawled along the short length of tunnel before turning right the way Jayne had come. The tunnel then turned left, and they could soon see the bottom of the shaft where it ended underneath the chicken hut. There was no chance of discovery with the chicken hut locked from the inside and Boff on watch above.

Jayne pushed the little wooden square above her head until dim light cascaded down into the shaft. Two indignant chickens sitting on eggs above them made gentle throaty noises as the two Naitabal heads appeared one at a time from the strange hole in the floor. Jayne and Ben lowered the trap-door into its recess, replaced the pile of earth, and dropped the second trap-door on top of that. They covered the whole thing with straw, and only then did they unlock the door of the chicken hut. Jayne glanced up at the Naitabal tree-house.

"No red flag," she said. "It's safe to go out."

Once inside the tree-house, Ben confirmed that Peter's secret letter was still safe. He and Jayne were brought up to date with the other news, and finally glanced into Boff's corner. Jayne asked the same question that Charlotte had asked.

"Hasn't Boff done it yet?"

Charlotte shook her head.

"No."

"It must be difficult, then, if Boff hasn't done it."

They all looked across at the advertisement that had appeared in the local paper two days before, and was now pinned to the wall in front of Boff. It said:

```
He/she who solves this
exquisite puzzle
should use the digits below
to check if it fits.
186945
```

No, it wasn't a Naitabal secret.

But unknown to the Naitabals, it soon would be.

## CHAPTER TWO

# *Code-breaker*

Boff didn't need to look at the advertisement any more. He had been working on it for two days, and had already written it out on his pad dozens of times, backwards, forwards and every way he could think of, but nothing that made any sense had emerged.

"I don't suppose it's the first letters?" Jayne suggested helpfully.

Boff flipped back the pages of his pad.

"No. That gives you 'hswstepsutdbtciif'. Complete nonsense."

"Last letters?" said Toby.

"'Eeosseedeeswokfts'," said Boff. "And I've tried middle letters, alternate first and last letters, second letters, third letters, and now I've started doing anagrams. It just won't make any sense."

"I think someone's done it for a joke," said Toby.

"No," said Ben, making his voice sound like a newsreader, "I bet it's a hidden message to a criminal gang that sparks off a series of events of world-shattering consequences. I bet it means 'set off the bomb on Tuesday' or 'set fire to London on Wednesday' or—"

"Or tie a gag on Ben's mouth," put in Charlotte, "preferably as soon as possible."

Ben grinned.

"There must be a reason for the advert, though," said Jayne. "People don't pay money to put big adverts like that in the paper for nothing."

"Has anyone tried ringing the number?" said Toby. "It

could be local."

"Yes," Boff confessed. "It's unobtainable. Anyway, all our local numbers begin with 8, not 1."

"There's an 8 in that one," said Toby. "Put the 8 at the front and mix the others up. Try all the combinations."

"I've already thought of that, too," said Boff. "Do you know how many combinations there are of five different digits? Well, I'll tell you – it's a hundred and twenty. I'm not going to ring a hundred and twenty numbers. Apart from the cost, what would I say to the person at the other end? I saw your advertisement, and I haven't actually solved it, but – ?"

"But you could *pretend* you've solved it," said Toby. "The person wouldn't know that you'd just called a hundred and nineteen others first."

"Help yourself if you fancy doing it," said Boff.

Toby shrugged.

"It was just an idea."

Jayne suddenly wrinkled her nose in suspicion.

"It's not an anagram of *Cedric's* number, is it?" she said.

"No," said Charlotte.

"What about the letters in Scrabble?" suggested Jayne.

"I tried them," said Boff. "You run out of S's, Z's and blanks before you've finished the first line."

"So that's no good, then."

"Keep the ideas coming, though," said Boff. "I'd love us to be the ones to solve it, but I'm beginning to think it's impossible."

"You need a break," said Ben. "That's what you need."

"There's no sign of the Igmopong," said Charlotte, brightening. "Let's go and finish building our raft."

Boff looked at the other Naitabals as if they were mad.

"I really want to solve this puzzle before I do anything more with the raft," he said. "If we don't do it today, someone will beat us to it. It's been in the newspaper for two days already. I don't want anyone else to solve it before we do."

"Why don't you ask the newspaper?" said Charlotte. "They might even tell you who put the advert in."

It seemed such a simple answer that Boff couldn't believe he hadn't thought of it himself.

"Wait here," he said.

Without further thought, Boff climbed through the trap-door in the roof, walked across the three-rope bridge to the oak on Boff Island, and disappeared into his house next door.

The others discussed the next stage of putting the finishing touches to their raft, and Boff returned a few minutes later.

"Well?" said Ben.

"They don't know who placed the advert. They said it didn't matter because it wasn't advertising goods, and as it was almost impossible to know what it meant, they just printed it."

"Didn't they see who placed it?" said Charlotte. "Didn't whoever-it-was write a cheque or something, or use a credit card?"

"No. I asked them. They said the ad came in an envelope with twice as much cash as it would cost, with a printed note telling them to give the rest to charity."

"It all sounds fishy to me," said Toby.

"It *is* fishy," said Boff. "That's all the more reason to solve it."

They all looked again at the advertisement pinned to the wall of the Naitabal hut:

```
He/she who solves this
exquisite puzzle
should use the digits below
to check if it fits.
186945
```

"You said you ran out of Scrabble letters," said Charlotte. "Why don't we get several Scrabble sets – we've all got one at home. We might see some sort of pattern?"

Boff was listening, but thinking at the same time.

"That's something I haven't tried," he said suddenly.

"What?"

Everyone was anxious to help Boff solve the puzzle now so that they could all go and finish the raft and try it out on the river. They knew Boff wouldn't come until he knew the answer.

Boff had turned to a new page of his big writing pad, and was writing the letters of the alphabet in a column.

Jayne, watching, said, "That reminds me."

"What does?"

"You writing the alphabet. How do you say the alphabet in Naitabal language?"

"That's easy," said Charlotte, who was the acknowledged expert on the subject. The word 'a' is *ang* in Naitabal language, isn't it?"

"Yes," said Jayne. "I know that already."

"And the word 'I' (meaning me), is *Ing*, isn't it . . ."

"Yes. I see. I hadn't thought of it like that."

"Well, that's it. The alphabet follows the same endings as the rest of Naitabal language. You can sing the Naitabal alphabet to the tune of 'Good King Wenceslas'."

Charlotte took a deep breath and sang:

"*Ang, bang, cang, dang,*

"*eng, feng, geng,*

"*heng, ing, jing, king, ling, ming,*

"*ning, ong, pong, quong, rong, song, tong,*

"*ung, vung, wung, xung, yung, zung.*"

"That's nice," Jayne laughed. "Yes, it is easy, isn't it?"

Behind them, Boff was still writing, but beginning to look impatient.

"Can we try and do *this* now?"

"No," said Charlotte firmly. "Jayne's a Naitabal just as much as the rest of us. It's our fault if we didn't teach her how to say 'BBC' in Naitabal language when she joined."

"I hadn't thought of that," said Jayne. "How *do* you say 'BBC' in Naitabal language?"

"*Bang,Bang,Cang*, of course," said Charlotte. "You use the alphabet for initials."

"Initialisms," murmured Boff under his breath.

"So the R.S.P.C.A. is the *Rong,Song,Pong,Cang,Ang*," said Toby, putting in one of his favourites.

"And the N.S.P.C.C. is the *Ning,Song,Pong,Cang,Cang*," said Ben, putting in one of his.

"And in cricket," said Toby, "you can be out *Ling,Bang,Wung*."

Jayne laughed, enjoying this new dimension of their secret language.

"But initial*isms* that spell *words*," put in Charlotte, glancing down her nose at Boff, "like NATO . . ."

"Are acronyms," said Boff. He tilted his head back this time and glanced along his nose horizontally at Charlotte, who continued:

"They're used like normal words, but they keep their capitals when you write them down. So NATO is *ATO-Ning*; and RoSPA is *oSPA-Rong*."

"Yes," said Boff. "And E.S.P. is *Eng,Song,Pong*, but I suppose you *knew* I was going to say that."

"Okay," said Charlotte, "very clever."

"Do you mean *Ong,King*?" said Toby.

"*Ong,King, Off-bang*," Charlotte continued. "What's this wonderful thing you haven't tried with this impossible advert?"

"I think I've done it now, in spite of the background noise," Boff murmured sarcastically, which was unusual for Boff. He held up his pad, then made his announcement. "There are six letters missing," he said.

"What do you mean, there are six letters missing?"

"Look." Boff showed her the list. "I took the message and crossed off each letter of the alphabet – just as we would if we'd been using Scrabble letters."

"So?"

"Well, there are six letters of the alphabet that haven't been used at all, that's all."

"What are they?"

Boff read them out.

"*Ang, Jing, Ming, Ning, Rong, Yung*," he said. "A, J, M, N, R and Y."

"But you could take any sentence and you'd get some letters left out," said Ben.

"Yes," said Boff. "But usually it's 'X' and 'Z' and 'Q' that don't get used."

Boff's brows furrowed again as he struggled with what it might mean.

"Perhaps they spell a word?" suggested Toby, glancing at the paper. "MARJYN; NARMYJ; JYMRAN . . ."

"JARMYN!" shouted Jayne. "That could be a surname, couldn't it? There's no *other* word you can get out of it!"

Boff said nothing. Instead, in silence, he repeated his earlier moves by climbing out of the escape hatch in the roof and disappearing along the three-rope bridge. When he returned a few minutes later he was carrying the local telephone directory. He dumped it down on the ledge.

"Well done, Jayne," he said. "There aren't any MARJYNs, NARMYJs or JYMRANs in the telephone book, but there are five 'Jarmyns'. He opened the page and showed them. "It's worth a try, but I don't fancy ringing them all. Anyway, it's got to be *certain*, not just chance."

Ben shrugged.

"We could ring one each," he said.

Now Jayne was staring at Boff's pad and the telephone book.

"Boff! Look!" She stabbed a finger on the page. "The telephone number for *that* Jarmyn has got the same digits as the ones in the advert – but they're in a different order!"

Boff looked where Jayne's shaking finger was pressing down on the phone book. Quickly, in alphabetical order, he wrote down the six missing letters on his pad. Then, underneath, he wrote the number from the advert:

```
A J M N R Y
1 8 6 9 4 5
```

"So," he said. It was unusual for Boff to show any emotion, but there was no mistaking the hint of excitement in his voice. "If we rearrange the letters and keep their numbers with them, we get . . ." and he wrote:

```
J A R M Y N
8 1 4 6 5 9
```

"And it matches the one in the phone book!" shouted Jayne.

There was no stopping them now. They rose as one body, locked the tree-house in record time, and all scrambled along the bridge to Boff Island. Minutes later they were in Boff's hall, and Boff's trembling hand was dialling the magic number 814659.

Three rings later, a voice answered. It was an educated male voice with a soft tone.

"Hello?"

"Is that Mr Jarmyn?" said Boff. He found that his voice was shaking now, as well as his hand.

"Yes."

"I know this sounds silly, but . . ." Boff stopped.

"Do go on, please."

"Well, we saw this advertisement in the local paper, and we think we've worked out what it really means. The missing letters spell your name, and the number is the same anagram if the missing letters are put back in alphabetic order, and – I'm sorry, I know it sounds stupid – but it's just a coincidence, isn't it?"

There was a horrible pause before the voice said, "No." It sounded as if it had a smile on it. "No, it's *not* a coincidence. Congratulations! You are the first person to find me. You sound so young, too. How old are you – may I ask?"

"*Nearly* thirteen," said Boff.

"My goodness!" There was a respectful silence. "I wondered if anyone would be clever enough to solve it, and yet it turns out to be a doddle for a twelve-year-old boy! Congratulations!"

"*Nearly* thirteen," Boff repeated, glowing with pleasure at the compliment.

"Did I hear you say 'we' solved it? Does that mean your parents helped you, then?"

"Oh, no. We did it ourselves – we all did it together. None of us could have done it on our own. Jayne was especially brilliant."

Boff turned to look at Jayne as she radiated happiness.

"And how old is Jayne? Is she your big sister? Eighteen? Twenty?"

"Jayne is ten."

"What!"

"I'm the oldest. We're just a group of friends. We like solving mysteries."

"Do you?" beamed the voice. "You sound the perfect solution to my problem, then."

"Your problem?"

"I suppose you want to know why I placed the advertisement?"

"Well, yes – please."

"I have a problem – a tricky problem. I wanted to find someone who liked solving horrendous problems, but I couldn't advertise in the usual way because I'd get swamped with calls from people who *think* they can solve problems but are really no good at solving them at all."

"Oh."

"So I thought a nice cryptic advertisement might do the trick – and here we are a week later, and it *has* done the trick, except—"

"Except we're too young . . ." said Boff, beginning to sound disappointed.

"Well, I must admit, I don't know that you'd be quite up to it. I was rather expecting to get a professor of cryptography . . ."

Boff's face suddenly became determined and serious.

"*And-ang ou-yung et-geng e-ming*," he said.

"Pardon?" said the voice.

"It's Naitabal language," said Boff, loftily, then added, "Don't you speak Naitabal language?" He knew perfectly well that there was a zero chance in ten million that Mr Jarmyn had heard of Naitabal language, and zero chance that he could speak it.

"Naitabal language?" said Mr Jarmyn, confused. "Where does that originate?"

"Naitagonia," said Boff, promptly.

Mr Jarmyn sounded flummoxed now.

"Is that one of the far eastern groups of islands?"

"I suppose it is," said Boff, with a ghost of a smile at the others, who were now crowded round the earpiece. "In a way."

There was a long pause, then Mr Jarmyn spoke again.

"You're *better* than a professor of cryptography aren't you? That's what you're trying to tell me?"

"Yes," said Boff, gently. "We'd like to solve your problem – please. Please give us a chance. You can always try someone else if we can't do it."

"Yes, but . . ." There was another short pause.

"*Please*, Mr Jarmyn."

"In some ways, I suppose, children might be better . . ."

"Just give us a week – or even a few days. If someone else solves the advert in the meantime you can use them instead."

There was another agonising silence, then Mr Jarmyn spoke decisively.

"Where can we meet?"

Suddenly, they had reached the most difficult part of the conversation. There was no way that they could go to the house of a complete stranger – it might be a dangerous trap. And they certainly weren't going to allow strangers inside the Naitabal tree-house, either – that was a privilege granted to only a few special adults, including Mr Elliott, who had built it for them.

"Do we have to meet?" said Boff. "Can't you just explain what the problem is on the telephone?"

There was another pause.

"I'd rather not. It's a cipher, you see," he said. "Something in code I found a long time ago. I haven't the faintest idea what it's about, and because it's in code, I've no way of knowing. It's been driving me mad for years, and I'm dying to know what it says. I don't want to trust it to the post in case it goes astray, and I don't want to say it over the telephone in case anyone listens in."

"Okay."

They agreed to meet in a safe public place – the park – in half an hour, then Boff replaced the receiver and related the entire conversation to the other Naitabals. They'd heard quite a lot of it already, because they'd been taking it in turns to press near to the ear-piece at Boff's side, and pick up the conversation at first hand.

Soon afterwards Toby announced that the Igmopong had returned to Pigmo Island.

"It sounds as if they're having an argument," he said.

"So what's new?" said Charlotte.

## CHAPTER THREE

# *Aft-rong*

"They're up to something," said Doris Morgan, "and I want to know what it is."

Cedric was nowhere to be seen, so his sister Doris had taken over his role as leader of the Igmopong.

"We *all* want to know what it is," breathed Amanda Wilson. "They're always up to *something*, and they always try to leave us out."

"Yeah," said Andy, who was pink and skinny, like a chipolata sausage. His sister Amanda was tubby, and looked as if she consumed three-quarters of their food, instead of half each.

Cedric's gang were known to the Naitabals as the Igmopong, but they called themselves The Fixers. The three members present were squatting on the sloping floor of their flimsy tree-house. They were forced to hang on the nearby branches to stop themselves being launched into empty air by the force of gravity.

They had regrouped after their failed attempts to follow the Naitabals, and were surprised that Cedric had still not reappeared. Even Doris didn't know where he was. She directed a question at Andy.

"What happened when you followed Charlotte?" she said.

"She went into the wood. She didn't see me, but my shoe lace came undone, and by the time I tied it, she'd gone."

There was a stunned silence.

"*You stopped to tie your shoe lace?*" barked Doris at last.

"Yeah. It was undone."

"Oh, good, I'm glad to hear that," said Doris sarcastically.

"I'm so relieved you didn't stop to tie it up when it *wasn't* undone." She exhaled a long-suffering sigh. "I'm surprised you didn't take some spare clothing with you and stop to change *that*."

Andy, who had apparently been inoculated against sarcasm at birth, had lost track of Doris's meaning.

"Do you want me to wear something without laces, then?" he said. "Like sandals, or wellingtons? And different clothes?"

Doris was too exasperated to reply, so Amanda seized the chance to file her own report.

"I watched Barry Offord and Jayne," she said. "Jayne went into the chicken place, but Boff didn't go anywhere. Then I saw Ben and Jayne climbing their rope ladder. I didn't see where Ben came from. I suppose he must have climbed over the fence."

"Cedric was supposed to be watching Ben," said Doris, finding the power of speech again (it never deserted her for long). "I followed Toby, of course, but he suddenly ran so fast I couldn't keep up without giving myself away. Hey! If Ben's back, how come Cedric isn't back as well?"

"I don't know," said Amanda.

"They're building something," Doris went on. "Andy saw Charlotte carrying rope, and I've seen Ben with planks of wood, and Jayne with chairs, and Toby had a big plastic drum today. I wonder what they're making?"

"Perhaps it's another tree-house," said Andy.

"Don't be stupid!" snapped Doris. "You don't use plastic drums to build a tree-house! You use plastic drums for—"

Doris stopped as a wonderful rush of inspiration came to her.

"You use plastic drums to make . . . a *raft*!" she shouted, clenching her fists in triumph. "That's it! I bet they're making a *raft*. Near the river. Why didn't we think of it before?"

"Because if we'd thought of it before, we couldn't have thought of it now, could we?" said Andy, logically.

"You—" Doris lost the ability to speak once again, but only for the usual few seconds. She turned to Amanda in the hope of getting some sensible responses. It always seemed much better, somehow, when Cedric was there to be shouted down. It was much easier pooh-poohing *his* ideas than trying to think up new ones of her own.

"I know what we can do!" she said, trying to avoid Andy's eye. "We'll find out where it is, and wait for 'em to finish making it, and then we'll hijack it!"

"That's piracy," said Andy.

"Yes," said Doris, staring him down. "And we'll hoist a skull and crossbones on it!"

"Where'll we get 'em?"

"We'll use real ones. Yours!"

Doris turned to Amanda again. "Then *we'll* have a raft, and they won't, and they won't be able to catch us because *we'll* be on the river, and they'll be on the bank. Unless they can walk on water . . ." she put in as an afterthought, "but I suppose the clever old stupid Naitabals think they can do that as well!"

Doris was so excited with her idea that she decided not to wait for Cedric any longer.

"Look!" she said. "The Naitabals are all back in their tree-house. We can go and find the raft now. It's bound to be near the river somewhere, isn't it? They wouldn't want to carry it for miles and miles."

"Good idea," said Amanda.

"Yeah!" said Andy.

"I'll just go and see if Cedric's in the house, then we can all go together." Doris released her grip on the branch and slid towards the precipice. She grabbed the rope that hung nearby and started lowering herself to the ground, talking as she went.

"I'll meet you in Gray's Wood by the entrance, but don't let any of the stupid old Naitabals see you! Hide! Otherwise they'll get suspicious and start following us." As she lowered her body to the ground, she lowered her voice to a whisper. "We don't want them to know we've found out where it is. It's got to be a secret. We'll let them finish building it, then grab it before they can even give it a maiden voyage!"

As Doris ran towards her house, Andy and Amanda loosened their grips and followed her back to earth.

Mr Jarmyn was about fifty years old, of medium build, with very thin close-cropped silvery hair, and clean-shaven. He stood up to greet the Naitabals with a smile, shaking their hands as they introduced themselves.

"Barry Offord."

"We call him 'Boff'. Charlotte Maddison."

"Toby Hamilton."

"Ben Tuffin."

"Jayne Croft."

The idea of meeting in the middle of a huge playing field in the public park had been Boff's. That way there was no danger of them being kidnapped, and no chance of anyone overhearing their conversation – especially the Igmopong.

They quite liked the look of Mr Jarmyn, but were still naturally cautious. They sat on the grass while Mr Jarmyn pulled a sealed envelope from his pocket.

"As I mentioned on the telephone, I found this in a bunch of letters that I was sorting out for a friend. The contents are in code. I was quite intrigued by it and I've been trying to crack it for years. I started the usual way, counting the number of occurrences of each letter, seeing if I could guess which ones were the letter 'E', and which ones were double, and so on. The strangest thing was there seemed to be similar quantities of all the letters, and that would never happen in an English sentence. So it didn't seem as if it would be a simple substitution of one letter for another.

"Then I bought a book on encoding and encrypting, and read about the German 'enigma' machine that was used during World War Two. It used a simple substitution method, but the look-up code changed every time you used a letter. As long as you knew how to do the same thing backwards, you could decode the messages, and that's exactly what our boffins managed to do. But these days, with computers, life is a lot more complicated. If this one's been done using a computer, we're probably sunk, but I don't think it was, somehow. I don't think it would have been handwritten if that was the case."

"What else did you try?" said Boff.

"Oh, everything I could find. I've tried for years and given up, now. That's why I placed the advertisement."

"*Your* code was pretty clever," said Jayne.

"I was lucky my name has all *different* letters of the alphabet, wasn't I?" said Mr Jarmyn, chuckling. "And even luckier that it has six letters – the same as the number of digits in my phone number."

"It didn't matter about those being different, of course," said Boff. "But what if the others hadn't been?"

"I'd have had to think of some other code, wouldn't I?" said Mr Jarmyn, and smiled at them all like a cheeky boy.

Boff was fingering the sealed envelope.

"It might take us a long time to do this," he said. "It took us two days to do yours."

"All you'll need is a bit of luck," said Mr Jarmyn. "Just pick on the right idea and test it out. As soon as something makes sense, you know you're on to a winner. If you manage to crack it, I'll give you a small reward – no promises, mind – it depends what it says. It might say something stupid like 'I bet it takes you years to crack this code, Ha, Ha'."

The Naitabals laughed, all except Boff, who was still feeling the envelope and thinking.

"There's one thing, though," Mr Jarmyn continued. He coughed slightly as if his words were causing some embarrassment. "I don't want you to say anything to anyone about this – whether you solve it or not."

"Why not?" said Boff, suddenly uneasy. "I mean, we wouldn't anyway, but—"

"We're good at keeping secrets," said Charlotte.

"We've got loads of them already," said Toby.

"Millions," said Jayne. "And we wouldn't tell anyone."

"Even if they tortured us," said Toby, "and pulled out our fingernails, and stretched us between two springy trees and cut the ro—"

"Thanks, Toby," said Charlotte reprovingly, then, turning to Mr Jarmyn, "We wouldn't tell anyone, but why did you say we shouldn't?"

"If you solve it, I'll tell you," came the answer. "But if you don't solve it, I'd rather you didn't show it to anyone else, ever."

"But why?" said Boff, still feeling uncomfortable.

"Because I'm doing it for a friend. It's not mine to splash around, you see. I told this friend that I'd do my best to solve it, and that I might try someone else really clever, but I'm not at liberty to let the whole world have a go. That's the very reason I didn't put the puzzle itself in *The Times* and let the whole nation try it out."

"I think I understand," said Boff. "We'll have a go, anyway, but we certainly won't give it to anyone else, so you don't need to worry."

They all stood up, then, and shook hands with their new acquaintance.

Back in the Naitabal tree-house, Boff waved the envelope in the air and gave his verdict.

"There's something suspicious about this," he said. "And I

don't trust Mr Jarmyn one centimetre."

The other Naitabals agreed that there was something fishy about it all.

"He changed his story," said Toby. "First he said he found it years ago, and then he said he was doing it for a friend."

"The only reason I can think of why he wouldn't want the whole world to have a try," said Charlotte, "is because there's something criminal about it."

But none of them could have realised just how shocking the contents would be – the last thing they ever could have imagined.

Charlotte was given the privilege of slitting open the envelope and extracting the single sheet of paper it contained. When she opened it out, they all saw the coded message written in a neat handwriting:

```
TNQBM HLVII ENQLF YUNEO SLVMQ RVKEG
TIVKG BBPOQ 24793 3TXGT YVVIZ SSHFX
```

It was exactly the same as the coded message that was hidden in their secret room – *the same secret message – unknown to anyone else – that Peter the Stranger had brought to them for safe keeping.*

## CHAPTER FOUR

# *Finders Keepers*

Cedric, his ear-drums still humming from his encounter with HMS *Slugface*, caught up with the other Igmopong as they were preparing to set off.

"Where have you been?" demanded Doris. "A fat lot of use *you* were, following Ben. He's been back *ages*."

"You'll have to speak up," said Cedric. "I've just been shouted half deaf by Mr Maynard."

"Oh, don't bother," said Doris. Instead, using sign language where necessary, she brought him up to date with what was happening. As soon as she'd finished, they noticed the Naitabals disappearing in the direction of the village. They couldn't believe their luck. It meant they were free to search for the Naitabals' raft without much risk of being caught. Cedric took the lead, and they hurried through the trees to the western limit of Gray's wood.

From there, walking along the edge of the river, they followed its northerly direction. They zigzagged in and out of the margin of the trees, examining every patch of undergrowth, and every place where a raft might be hidden. They were halfway along the stretch of river that bordered the wood, and fifty metres from its bank, when they found it. It was hidden in a hollow concealed by a dense thicket. They had difficulty finding the way in at first, so even Doris admitted grudgingly that it was a good hiding place.

"You'd never see it unless you were really looking for it," she said.

Cedric could hardly contain his excitement at finding the raft so quickly.

"Let's go in and have a closer look," he breathed.

A thorough examination of the raft revealed that it was not only well made, but just about finished. The hull was twelve white plastic drums, lashed with plastic strapping to two short ladders that ran the length of the vessel and served as an open deck. Four wooden chairs had had their legs removed, and were lashed to the ladders at each corner of the raft as rowing positions. There was plenty of space in between the chairs for more passengers or luggage. The middle of the raft was open space.

All four of them ran their hands over it, feeling its lines.

"Humph!" said Doris. "It hasn't got a sail."

"Or an engine," said Amanda.

"Or a lifeboat," said Andy.

"It's better than I thought it'd be, though," admitted Doris at last.

"But not as good as we'd've done it," said Cedric.

"No," said Andy. "Not as good as that."

"But it's good enough – I mean it'll save us actually making one, won't it?"

"Yes," said Cedric. "Now we've found it, we'll have to hide it from *them*."

"Yeah," said Andy.

"We could sail it down the river," said Amanda, "and find a new hiding place on the other side where they'd *never* find it."

All four of the Igmopong were suddenly gripped with an excitement that they hadn't felt for weeks. The idea of launching themselves on to an untamed river on a home-made raft was so exciting that they could hardly speak.

Somehow, they found the patience and skill it needed to pull the craft up out of the hollow, negotiate the tangled undergrowth, and drag it to the river bank.

It took them fifteen minutes, impeded mainly by their own habit of quarrelling about everything. They quarrelled over each detail of its movement, argued over how to lift it, and squabbled over how it should be launched into the river. But they still had the presence of mind to argue in whispers. They knew there was a very real danger that the Naitabals might appear at any moment and throw them into the water.

"We need a rope to hold it while we climb in," said Doris, when they had it poised above the bank.

"No, we don't," hissed Cedric. "I'll hold it while you all get on, and then I'll jump on."

"And what happens when we want to get off, Pirate Face?" Doris demanded quietly. "I suppose you'll jump off and leave the rest of us floating down the river?"

Cedric considered.

"All right. We need a rope, then. Let's untie one of these."

"That one's helping to hold the raft together."

"No, it isn't."

"What's it there for, then? A washing line?"

"Yeah. What's it there for?" said Andy.

Cedric thought again.

"What about this one, then?"

"That one looks just as important as the other one," sneered Doris. "Otherwise they wouldn't have bothered to tie it there, would they?"

After more argument, Andy was sent to look for ropes in the place where they'd found the raft. He came back in triumph a few minutes later holding up the coils of blue nylon rope that they had seen Charlotte carrying earlier in the day.

"Got some!" he shouted, then nearly tripped himself up with it.

They tied one rope to each end of the ladders, then Andy and Cedric held one each while Doris and Amanda pushed the raft over the edge of the bank and on to the water. The river was ten metres wide, but hardly moving, so there was no discernible current. Doris and Amanda climbed aboard, rolled up their jeans, removed their trainers and socks, and bagged the two front seats. They dangled their legs in the water.

"It feels really good," said Amanda.

Andy was next, taking the rope with him, and Cedric climbed on last.

"The Naitabals'll be really sick when they find their precious raft gone," he said.

"I wonder what they'll say?" said Andy.

"I bet they'll guess it's us," said Amanda.

"We'll have to park it on the other side of the river, so they can't get it," said Doris.

"I think you mean moor it," said Amanda.

"Pinching it was as easy as falling off a—" Cedric started to say. But as he said it, Doris and Amanda decided to change seats, and the raft wobbled violently. He was still standing up, and was almost hurled head first into the river. It was only by grabbing Andy's head that he saved himself.

" – raft?" Doris finished for him.

"Keep still, can't you?" Cedric hissed, picking himself up, but he was more surprised than hurt.

By this time the raft had begun to drift away from the river bank, propelled by Cedric's flying weight as he had jumped aboard. When they reached the middle of the river, the current started moving them downstream at a surprising rate.

"The river didn't seem very fast when we were on the bank," said Cedric nervously. "But it's going quite quick now, isn't it?"

They watched the bank with suspicion. It seemed to be speeding past them at an alarming rate, and it was only now that they realised that something vital was missing. It was Doris who spotted it.

"We haven't got any oars," she said.

The others looked around helplessly. The first exhilaration

they had felt disappeared rapidly as they took it in turns to mention some of the problems they hadn't dared think about before setting off.

"We haven't got a rudder, either," said Cedric. "We can't steer the stupid thing."

"I can't swim," said Amanda, starting to cry, "and we haven't got any l-life j-jackets. My d-dad said I must never, ever g-go on water without a l-life j-jacket."

"Why didn't you say so, then?" said Cedric, annoyed.

"I f-f-f-forgot."

"A fat good time to start forgetting," said Cedric, "now that we're *hurtling down the river out of control*."

These words and the panic in Cedric's voice only made matters worse. Amanda's crying redoubled.

"We haven't got any brakes, either," said Andy, unhelpfully. "We can't stop."

"And we d-don't know wh-where we're g-going," Amanda screamed.

Cedric looked back up the river. He was surprised to discover that their launch site was still visible upstream.

"We've only moved about twenty metres!" he snapped. "Anyone would think we'd been hurtling down white-water rapids for six hours, not floating on a stagnant river for two minutes."

Amanda stopped sobbing, looked up, and seemed to take some comfort from this sobering fact.

"I still can't swim," she said, in a last plea for attention.

"Well, *don't fall in*, then," said Doris, heartlessly. "If you do, you won't be rescued, because none of *us* can swim, either. Except we don't make a *fuss* about it."

Amanda started sobbing again until she noticed that they were drifting towards the opposite bank.

"Look!" she said. "We can get off there!"

"No we can't," said Cedric, assuming command again. "The Naitabals would see the raft there. We've got to take it down the river a *long way*, not just a few stupid metres."

Andy, meanwhile, was lying flat on his stomach between the chairs at the back and looking into the water in the middle of the raft.

"I can see the bottom," he announced.

"Where?" said Doris automatically, and regretted it.

Cedric let out a wild hoot of laughter and announced in a loud voice to the others that Doris wanted to know where the bottom of the river was. Doris turned a bright pink as the others giggled at her expense.

"It's not very deep," said Andy at last. "If anyone fell in, they could walk."

The others took it in turns to look over the side, and were relieved to see that Andy was right.

"That's one of our worries out of the way, then," said Doris, getting her own back. "If we get into trouble, we can put Andy in the water. He's the tallest."

"You'd float better," Andy mumbled.

The raft continued its journey down the river, drifting from one bank to the other in a majestic waggle, completely out of control.

They were almost a mile downstream when the raft discovered a submerged log and came to an abrupt and unexpected halt in the middle of the river. Doris and Amanda shot out of their seats and fell on Cedric, which probably saved him from being shot into the water, and Andy went sprawling into the chairs from behind. After sorting themselves out, they managed to lever the raft sideways.

What was turning out to be a nightmare ended when they drifted up against a paddock on the far side, and Cedric jumped off with rope in hand and secured the raft.

"Come on. Everybody off," he said. "We'll leave it here."

The others pretended to be sorry to get off, but were secretly relieved to be on dry land again. They hauled the raft into a hollow that couldn't be seen from the river, then started walking towards a house they could see in the distance.

Another trip into the Naitabal tunnel confirmed that the coded message that Mr Jarmyn had handed over was identical to the coded message that Peter had so recently given into their care. The only difference was that the one Mr Jarmyn had produced was in a different handwriting – probably Mr Jarmyn's – perhaps copied from another version of the original.

"The question is," said Charlotte, "what do we do now? Peter asked us to leave it alone, and not to bother to solve it."

"I don't see how we *can* leave it alone," said Ben. "If this Mr Jarmyn's got hold of a copy, it'll only be a matter of time before he gets someone else to solve it if we don't."

"But where could Mr Jarmyn have got it from?" said Boff. "The original piece of paper was sent to the Bad Man about the time Peter was born. It was only because his mother opened it first and hid it that the Bad Man never got it. The man who'd sent it died a day later in police custody."

"He must have sent a copy to someone else as well, then," said Jayne.

"If he did," said Toby, "why has the other person waited fourteen years before doing something about it?"

There was a pause.

"Perhaps he's just come out of prison," said Ben suddenly.

There was a stunned silence. Everyone was impressed.

"Mr Jarmyn, perhaps?" said Boff. "That's an idea. Except that Peter's letter said no one else was involved in whatever crime it was in the first place. And the man who died sent the code to the Bad Man so they would both know where he'd hidden whatever-it-was."

"The thing is," said Charlotte, "do we go ahead and crack the code, or not?"

"We ought to tell Peter."

"It's too dangerous," said Ben. "He asked us not to contact him, unless it was really vital. In case he's being watched. It might lead the Bad Man to *us*. It's too dangerous, much too dangerous. That's why he wrote the letter and gave us the secret stuff. No one will ever find it if there's no connection."

"But someone *has* found it – at least, a copy," said Boff. "But I agree – it's not vital – not yet."

"All the more reason to solve it before anyone else does," said Jayne, "without wasting any more time."

The Naitabals didn't need any more reasons. They set to work with a vengeance, going straight to the library to borrow a book on secret codes. Then they armed themselves with pencils and fat notebooks, locked themselves into the Naitabal hut, and started work.

They all copied the code carefully, making sure they didn't make any mistakes:

```
TNQBM HLVII ENQLF YUNEO SLVMQ RVKEG
TIVKG BBPOQ 24793 3TXGT YVVIZ SSHFX
```

"The only letters that aren't used are A, C, D, J, and W," said Ben after a bout of ticking with his pencil. "And there are six 'V's and four 'I's, 'Q's and 'T's. All the other letters are used one, two or three times."

"I'm not sure what to make of that," said Boff, doing some scribbling of his own.

"It's funny that all the words are five letters," said Jayne.

"I wouldn't pay much attention to that," said Boff. "Some codes are set out that way because you're supposed to make up columns and rows. Otherwise, it's just a method of writing it so you don't give away clues about simple words, like 'a' and 'I'."

And those were the last words the other Naitabals heard

from Boff for the rest of the morning. It was as if he had gone to a different planet.

They all tried hundreds of ways of cracking the code. In Boff's corner the pencil flew back and forth like a weaver's shuttle, and the pages of his pad turned regularly as if he was doing five hundred lines.

Meanwhile, Charlotte was making two paper wheels, one slightly smaller than the other. She wrote the alphabet on each, spaced evenly round the edge, and then pinned the wheels together at the hub. By rotating the smaller wheel, she could line up any letter with any other letter. She explained quietly to the others, except Boff, who was still on his distant world.

"Look, I can use twenty-six starting positions for the first letter of the code, 'T'. I might start it against 'A'. Then I turn the wheel one to the left, and look up the second letter of the code, 'N'. If it starts making sense, I'll carry on. If it doesn't, I'll start again in a new position. When I've done all the starting positions I'll try turning it to the right instead. And when I've done those, I can turn it two to the right, or three."

"It'll take years," said Toby, and suddenly looked sleepy.

"We've got to try," said Charlotte, making a start.

At one o'clock, Boff gave an audible groan and slumped over his pad.

"Boff's had it," said Jayne. "So have I. I'm not getting anywhere."

"The numbers just make it even more confusing," said Ben. "Not that I've solved any of the letters."

"I think it's impossible," said Toby.

"I think it's a hoax," said Ben. "I bet Mr Jarmyn is Cedric Morgan's uncle, and I bet Cedric made up the code so that we'd spend hours and hours trying to solve it, and all the time it's just nonsense."

Suddenly Toby's face clouded over.

"I've just thought of something horrible," he said.

"What?"

"Ben might be right about Cedric and the code, or he might not."

"So?"

"Well – we haven't seen the Igmopong for hours. If it *is* a trick, I hope they haven't spent all this time *looking for our raft*."

CHAPTER FIVE

# *Naitabals Never Tell Lies*

Toby's words came crashing into the Naitabals like an avalanche, sweeping away all thoughts of the secret code. Even Boff managed to find the energy to turn his head and look at the others aghast.

"They *have* been horribly quiet," breathed Charlotte.

There was an ominous silence until Toby hauled himself to his feet.

"I'll go and check," he said quietly. "We haven't been near the raft for ages. Anything might have happened."

"I'll come as well," said Ben.

"We'll all go," said Charlotte and Jayne together. "Boff?"

Boff eased himself into an upright position.

"Yes, I'll come. I think a break from the code will do us good."

Fifteen minutes later they were standing in a ragged group, gazing in despair into the empty hollow where their raft had been. There was no doubt in anyone's mind as to who had taken it.

"I hope they all drown," said Charlotte. "Beasts."

"I want to know how they managed to find it," said Toby. "None of them ever followed me here. I always made a million per cent sure I'd shaken them off before I came in this direction."

"Just their usual luck, probably," said Jayne. "It'll be just their luck to survive the river, as well.

"Drowning's too good for them," said Ben. "It's too quick."

"I hadn't replaced that leaky drum yet," said Toby. "It won't make it sink, but it might be a bit lop-sided."

Boff shrugged.

"Never mind," he said, dismissing it. "We'll build another one. There's plenty more plastic drums and rope and wood in the Sea of Debris. We'll build it there and guard it. It doesn't matter if they see it now, does it? Not now that the secret's out."

He turned and started walking back.

"I'm going to have another go at the code," he said over his shoulder, and was gone.

"I've never seen Boff looking so tired," said Charlotte, watching him go.

"It's the code," said Ben. "Mental energy is the most tiring, and Boff's been really concentrating on it."

"I hope he cracks it," said Jayne. "Because I don't think I ever will."

"I don't think I will, either," said Toby. "If Boff can't do it, I don't know who can."

They turned and looked at the raft's last resting-place again, hoping that some miracle might have made it reappear while their backs had been turned. But all they saw was a raft-size patch of flattened weeds.

"Let's go to the river," said Ben, "and see if we can see it."

"Or the Igmopong," said Jayne.

"Or their bodies," said Toby, hopefully.

Moments later, they were standing near the water's edge. Upstream, the river curved sharply to the left, out of sight. To their right, downstream, they were greeted by an empty expanse of slow-moving water. No raft. No Igmopong. No bodies.

"They won't have gone upstream," said Jayne, "unless they brought their own paddles."

"And if they've gone downstream without paddles, they won't be coming back upstream, either," said Charlotte.

"What we need," said Ben, "is another raft. And quick."

The others caught his mood.

"Come on!" said Toby. "Let's go and make it now, while the Igmopong are out of the way. I bet they won't be back for hours."

In the Sea of Debris, there was no sign of Boff. The Naitabal hut was locked and silent.

Mrs Morgan saw them arrive and waddled across Pigmo Island towards them, looking anxious.

"Have any of you seen Cedric and Doris?" she asked. "I haven't seen any sign of them for ages."

"Sorry," said Charlotte. "We haven't." She wondered whether to tell Mrs Morgan that her precious son and daughter were at that moment risking their lives up an uncharted creek without a paddle, but decided against it. It wouldn't do Mrs Morgan's heart any good, and she was famous for having the screaming hab-dabs. The only thing that was nagging the back of Charlotte's mind was that none of them could swim. "We haven't seen them since early this morning."

Mrs Morgan wrung her apron in her hands.

"It's unusual for them not to come back for lunch," she said.

"I bet it is, too," Jayne murmured to Toby.

"I'm sure they'll turn up soon," said Charlotte.

"Wet," whispered Ben.

"What did you say?" said Mrs Morgan. Her radar had picked up Ben's voice in the background.

"Y-yet," said Ben. "We haven't seen them *yet*."

"Oh, thank goodness. I thought for a minute you said 'wet'. Never mind. If you see them, will you tell them to hurry up?"

"Okay," said Charlotte.

The Naitabals went to their homes for food. When they met up again, without Boff, they set to work on the new raft.

With Mr Elliott's garden full of forty years' worth of builder's junk, there was never much difficulty in finding what they wanted. They picked their way over the abandoned heaps of wood and bricks, furniture, solidified cement bags and general trash, and pulled out another twelve plastic drums. No one knew why Mr Elliott had got so many, but they were certainly perfect for raft-making. Charlotte fetched some super-glue and used it to screw up the bungs to stop water getting in, and air getting out. The others sawed an old ladder in half and strapped the drums in rows to each piece using Mr Elliott's plastic strapping machine.

Every five minutes Mrs Morgan came out looking more and more worried, asking if they'd seen any sign of her precious children. The answer was just as negative, and they assured her each time that they would tell her as soon as they saw anything.

Naitabal raft Mark 2 progressed rapidly.

"Gosh, it's much quicker making it here than when we had to sneak everything into the woods," said Jayne. "It was a nuisance having to avoid the Igmopong."

"It was murder having to do it quietly," said Charlotte, "crouched down in that dark hollow."

It was true. It only took them an hour and half to strap the drums to the ladders, and another half an hour to tie the ladders together with battens that would also hold the seats.

"Now for the chairs," said Ben.

A few minutes later, Mrs Morgan came out of her back door again. She hurried across to the fence, but this time her face was creased in smiling furrows like a potato field.

"Cedric telephoned from someone's house!" she said. "And they're safe!"

Charlotte suppressed an inner groan. She wouldn't have cared if the Igmopong had disappeared for ever, but she was still curious to know where they'd got to.

"Where were they?" she said, trying not to sound too interested.

"Those naughty children!" Mrs Morgan said proudly. "Do you know what they've done?"

"No . . ." said Charlotte.

"They built themselves a raft! And they've sailed it on the river! All by themselves! Aren't they clever?"

Charlotte opened her mouth to protest, but her words were paralysed at birth.

"Of course," Mrs Morgan hurried on, "it was *very* naughty of them to go without telling us," – her face dropped for a moment – "and I shall have words to say about that . . ."

The Naitabals stood transfixed as Mrs Morgan's beaming smile returned, and she continued on her verbal gallop.

"I'm so *proud* of them," she went on. "They've been building this raft for *weeks* in the woods without telling a *soul*. Daddy and I never *guessed!* And today they launched it and sailed it down the river for more than a mile! They've parked it in someone's field. And the man who lives there was so *impressed* with their own home-made raft, he offered to bring them home to save them a long walk. But Daddy's gone to get them. Aren't they *clever* little darlings?"

Mrs Morgan took a huge breath, and seemed to notice for the first time that the Naitabals were less than impressed.

"Oh, look!" she declared. "You're all *jealous!* Cedric must have *told* you about their wonderful idea, and . . ." her eyes travelled to the new structure at their feet, "and you're making a raft of your own! Copying Cedric!" She chuckled, enjoying herself. "I bet yours won't be as good as his!"

Still in a trance of delight, she spun girlishly on her heel and trotted back into her house, flapping her hands like butterfly wings and murmuring, "A whole mile! On their own raft! I'm so proud of them!"

The Naitabals, bereft of the power of speech by Cedric's audacity, remained in silent shock for several more seconds.

They all felt physically sick. Gradually, they started to give vent to their feelings. Jayne was the first to explode.

"Cheek! Of all the cheek! I can't believe it!"

"*Right!*" muttered Ben. "That's *it*, Cedric Morgan! You've *had* it!"

"I don't know how he can do it!" spluttered Charlotte.

"Well, he has," said Toby.

After several more minutes of venting their feelings, they flung themselves into finishing the new raft with redoubled vigour. Charlotte and Toby furiously sawed legs off chairs, pretending they were Igmopong legs, while Jayne and Ben lashed off-cuts to old broom handles to make paddles.

Not much later they heard a car draw up in the road outside, followed by the banging of doors. Soon afterwards, Cedric sidled into his back garden, keeping his beaming mother close by. The rest of the Igmopong followed at a safe distance.

"Have you heard about our raft?" Cedric called to the Naitabals in a loud voice. "We sailed it a whole mile down the river."

"Isn't he wonderful?" put in Mrs Morgan, still beaming. "Aren't they all clever?"

Every one of the Naitabals wanted to say, "It was our raft, not Cedric's", but each of them knew it would be completely useless. In fact, it would make things worse. It would make the Naitabals sound like cheats and sink them down to Cedric's level.

"We're going to put a mast on it next," Cedric announced. "And then a sail."

"And a rudder," said Doris.

"And paddles," said Amanda.

"And an engine," said Andy.

"No, we're not having an engine," Cedric snapped. "That was just Andy's joke. But Mummy's going to buy us life-jackets tomorrow. Aren't you?" he added, turning to her.

"Yes, darlings. It's very dangerous on rivers, even if they look really slow-moving."

"Sometimes those ones are *more* dangerous," Cedric butted in. "The river was *very* slow moving today."

"It was *very* naughty of Cedric and Doris and Andy and Amanda to go on the river without life-jackets," Mrs Morgan went on, "and they must *never* do it again."

All the while, Doris stood just behind Mrs Morgan making triumphant faces at the speechless Naitabals, daring them to say something. But they knew if they did, it would only get them a tongue-lashing from Mrs Morgan, "You wicked, selfish children, trying to spoil poor Cedric and Doris's fun!" None of them wanted to be humiliated in front of the Igmopong. After all, they couldn't *prove* that they had made the raft, so it was the Igmopong's word against theirs.

Their only consolation came when Mrs Morgan tried to give Cedric a nice big hug, and he resisted it by going stiff like a plank.

"Cedric's such a *sensitive* boy," Mrs Morgan said proudly, drooling over him. "He *loves* his hugs in the house, but he never lets me hug him in the garden!"

Cedric flushed bright pink and retreated hastily, dragging his mother and his cronies indoors. The Naitabals allowed themselves a consolation smile, and made a mental note for the future.

By teatime the raft was finished, but there was still no sign of Boff.

"I hope he's all right," said Ben.

"He's working on the code, that's all," said Jayne. "He just wants to concentrate."

"How are we going to stop the Igmopong getting to the new raft?" said Toby.

"I don't think they'll bother," said Charlotte, "now they've got one of their own."

"Now they *think* they've got one of their own," corrected

Ben. "But we'll chain ours up and padlock it just in case."

They decided not to disturb Boff for the rest of the evening, hoping that his absence meant he was making good progress on the code.

"He's got that book on secret codes to read through, and then he's got to test them all out," Ben reminded them.

They didn't see Boff again that day, and he didn't even respond at bedtime when they flashed their usual good nights in Naitabal Morse.

They were shocked when they discovered him the next morning. Ben went with the spare key to open the padlock on the roof of the Naitabal hut and soon saw that Boff was already inside. He was slumped across the ledge in his favourite corner, fast asleep. Ben signalled to the others to come in through the roof for once, and they all made their way quietly across the three-rope bridge and joined Ben inside.

Boff's glasses had fallen on to the floor, but hadn't broken. Scores of sheets of paper were scattered in every direction, and there were several strange wheels that Boff had obviously made – like Charlotte's – to make the business of looking up letters and codes that much easier. There were also sliders and tables and matrixes of letters and numbers. But there wasn't a single piece of paper with any words on it that made sense in English. There were several apple cores, two untouched oranges, three chocolate wrappers, a single sandwich, and an empty milk bottle.

"He's been here all night," Ben said in a hushed voice.

"It doesn't look as though he's solved the code," Jayne whispered. "If he had, he'd have written it up in huge letters for all of us to see."

Trying not to disturb him, they tidied up the mess as best they could, but couldn't tidy the things Boff had gone to sleep on.

Charlotte took a blank sheet of paper and wrote on it in big letters 'WE'VE MADE ANOTHER RAFT!' She propped it up on the shelf near Boff's head, using his glasses to keep it in place. Then she pointed to the escape hatch in the roof, and they all departed to put the finishing touches to their new creation.

The raft hadn't been touched. Jayne's theory was that Cedric had probably been exhausted, gone to bed early, and was probably still there now. She wasn't wrong.

It was ten o'clock before Boff reappeared. The others had done more work on the raft, including places to store fresh water and food, a first aid kit, and emergency lifelines. All four of them were bent down fixing a flag pole into its slot when they became conscious of a bedraggled figure standing behind them.

It was Boff.

"I've given up," he said. "I can't do it. It's impossible."

"Boff, you can't give up!" said Charlotte, sounding distressed. She had never known Boff give up on anything. None of them had.

Boff smiled a weak smile.

"I've been at it half yesterday and half the night," he said. "I've tried every scheme in the book, and scores of my own. None of them work. It's impossible. We'll see Mr Jarmyn tomorrow and give him back his piece of paper."

## CHAPTER SIX

# *Except When Absolutely Necessary*

Up in the privacy of the Naitabal hut, they tackled Boff again.

"Boff, you can't give up!" begged Charlotte.

"It's not like you!" said Toby.

"Naitabals never give up!" said Jayne. "I'm sure we can solve it between us if we really try."

"You say you've tried everything in the book," said Ben. "What about the code that Mr Jarmyn used – leaving out letters of the alphabet – ?"

"I tried that."

"Was it in the book?"

"No, of course not."

"Well, that's it, isn't it?" said Ben. "*That* method wasn't in the book, but you thought of that. Forget the book. Think of something else."

"You write *any* sentence," said Boff, "the same length as that sentence in the code, and you *never* get the letters used so evenly."

"How about 'The quick brown fox jumps over the lazy dog"?' said Charlotte, trying to be helpful.

"That's an exception."

"This could be an exception."

"No. It means the code must be something like the enigma machine, and that's horrendously difficult. You've got to hit on exactly the right start, and exactly the right alphabet shifts . . . Perhaps the numbers in the middle of the code tell you to change the shift pattern every time . . . *It's just not possible.*"

The others had never seen Boff in such a mood. They were used to him working quietly in the corner while all sorts of things went on around him. He would even correct them about things when he was supposed to be concentrating, and always, always, he would come up with some sort of answer.

"Can't we ask your dad to help?" suggested Jayne.

"No. We promised we wouldn't tell anyone."

"But we can't just *give up*."

"We've only had it just under a day," said Toby. "We didn't tell Mr Jarmyn how long it would take. We know it's over thirteen years old already, and no one seems to have solved it in that time."

"Exactly," said Boff. "And I'm not going to spend thirteen years until I'm nearly twenty-six failing to solve it, either."

"Boff," Charlotte pleaded, "this is so unlike you. Aren't you just tired after being up most of the night? Won't you feel differently tomorrow, or the next day?"

"No. It's too difficult."

They argued and made suggestions for another half an hour, but Boff was unmoved. He didn't lose patience with them for badgering him, but just remained calm, parrying their questions. At the end, the answer was always the same, "It's too difficult."

Reluctantly, they allowed him to contact Mr Jarmyn.

Boff's voice on the telephone was just as calm.

"Mr Jarmyn? It's Barry Offord. We've all racked our brains all day and all night, and we can't solve the code, I'm afraid. I wondered if we could meet at the same place at eleven o'clock this morning, and I can give you your paper back . . . Oh, all right . . . Twelve o'clock, then. See you. Bye."

"Couldn't we just post it back?" said Charlotte as soon as Boff had replaced the receiver. "It'd be much easier."

"He doesn't want it trusted to the post in case it goes astray and someone sees it."

"We don't all need to go, though," Charlotte continued, sounding relieved.

"Yes, we do," said Boff. "All of us."

"What?"

"What do you mean?"

"Why?"

"Please. I'm very tired. Just please come with me and hand back the note. Let's just say I'd like you all to be witnesses that I hand back the note."

The other four Naitabals stared at Boff. His behaviour was so peculiar, it was almost as if they were speaking to a different person.

"But, Boff—"

"I'm going back to my house to get some breakfast and a bit of sleep," he said, ignoring any further protests. "I'll meet you at the skip at ten to twelve. Okay?"

The others nodded.

"Okay."

When he had gone, it was Charlotte who spoke first.

"I know Boff keeps things to himself sometimes," she said, "until he's sure about his ideas, but—"

"I know what you mean," said Ben. "This time he's so sure about not being able to do it, it seems almost odd. And to want us all to go and be *witnesses* . . ."

"Why doesn't he just tell us what's on his mind?" said Jayne, exasperated.

"I know what's happened," said Toby.

"What?" said the others.

"He's thought it all through, I think – about the code. The fact that it's the same message that we've hidden in the tunnel . . . Peter's code."

"And?"

"He's thought it through, and he doesn't *want* to solve the code. He thinks if he solves that code – *whatever it says* – it will land us in such a big, bad, nasty crime that we'll have the really big, bad, nasty criminals after us. He's afraid of what we'll get into. I think he's decided to give up before we're in it too deep. It's not that the code is impossible – I'm sure Boff could solve it eventually – but he's decided to make it impossible. And he wants Mr Jarmyn to know we've given up – really given up."

It was a long speech for Toby. But the others thought that he might be right. It was the only explanation so far for Boff's peculiar behaviour.

Perhaps, for the first time, they were seeing Boff afraid.

Mr Jarmyn greeted them with less of a smile than before, and it was clear he was disappointed.

"Well, I was very sorry to receive your telephone call, Barry. I really thought you would come up with the goods."

"I'm sorry. We've tried everything. We all spent most of yesterday on it, and I was up all night. I've read *Code-breakers*, and tried every device in the book. It doesn't fit anything. I can't make sense out of any little bit. I think you need the enigma machine."

Mr Jarmyn looked at them all closely.

"How do I know you haven't kept a copy of this?" he said suddenly, sounding irritated. "Because the rule of confidentiality still goes, you know."

Boff reached inside his shirt, produced a huge bundle of papers, and handed them over to Mr Jarmyn.

"There," he said. "That's all the copies that all of us were working on. It includes all our notes and all our try-outs, and even code wheels for looking up shifts in the alphabet. I promise – we have no copy of your piece of paper. And I certainly can't remember any of it, either."

Mr Jarmyn took the bundle of papers and seemed relieved.

"I think you've done the right thing," he said. "I'm afraid I've used you, but you're still the only people who replied to my advert in the local paper. There aren't many geniuses around, apparently. Perhaps whatever it says in this coded note is either meaningless, or highly dangerous. Either way, it would be wrong to waste any more time on it, especially for children."

With that, Mr Jarmyn walked slowly across the field and disappeared. The Naitabals headed slowly back towards Naitabal territory.

At the edge of the park, Mr Jarmyn stopped, turned, and took out a pair of binoculars.

None of the Naitabals said anything until they were safely inside the Naitabal hut, and this time it was Jayne who spoke first.

"We all think you could have solved it, Boff," she said, "so you mustn't feel bad about it. Toby thinks you don't *want* to solve it – because you think it might be dangerous . . . You don't want us to get into something nasty . . . Is that it?"

"No," said Boff. "The most important thing was to convince Mr Jarmyn that we *couldn't* solve it. If he thought for one moment that we had . . ."

"*What*, Boff?"

"I think Mr Jarmyn knows more about that piece of paper than he's telling us. I mean, how did he get it? He says he found it. Well . . . he must have found it in some situation that had 'hidden treasure' written all over it, otherwise why would he go to all the trouble to place that advert and try and get someone to solve it for him? As far as I can see, he must know that the code has a crooked origin – and the only way he'd know *that* is if he's a crook himself. I reckon he's just come out of prison – like Ben said – and someone gave him that code – or his accomplice gave it to him thirteen-plus years ago, and he's been itching to get out of gaol and find whatever-it-is ever since."

"So you think it's too dangerous to bother with?" said

Toby.

"I think Mr Jarmyn might be too dangerous to bother with." Boff paused and looked round at all their faces. "Do you think we convinced him?" he said at last.

"Why shouldn't we have convinced him?" said Charlotte. "You didn't crack the code, so that's all there is to it. Why on earth *shouldn't* he be convinced?"

Boff looked up quickly. His glasses caught a brief flash of light from the windows as he smiled and delivered his stunning news.

"Because I *did* crack the code," he said.

## CHAPTER SEVEN

# *Tong Lus-pong Ning Is-ing Heng*

"What?"

"Boff, but you said—"

"I'm sorry I had to lie to you," said Boff apologetically. "But don't you see it was necessary – really necessary?"

"*Naitabals never tell lies*," chanted Jayne, remembering her swearing-in as a Naitabal not so very long ago, "*. . . unless it's absolutely necessary . . .*"

"But why, Boff?" said Charlotte, who seemed the most hurt. "Why was it absolutely necessary?"

Boff's face was serious as he answered.

"You all agreed that Mr Jarmyn was convinced, didn't you?"

"Yes."

"Did you notice how he looked closely at each of you in turn, and you all looked genuinely down in the dumps?"

"Yes."

"Well, if I'd told you I'd solved it, we'd never have pulled it off. It was easier for me to act it out, knowing that I'd told you all a big lie. *But if I'd told you the truth, not all of us would have convinced him.* One of us might have given it away – it doesn't matter who. Mr Jarmyn would have seen it. It's impossible for five people to tell the same lie. As it was, I was the only one who had to lie to him. Do you see now? I made it easier for all of *you*."

"Well, why didn't you just tell us, and then go and see him on your own?" said Jayne. "Why did you make the rest of us go as well?"

"Because I wanted him to be one hundred per cent

convinced – *by all of us* – that we hadn't solved it, that's why. If he thinks for a moment we were bluffing him, or cheating him, I don't know what might happen. This could be dangerous, and I don't want Mr Jarmyn thinking for one second that we've cracked it. Do you understand now?"

"I think so," said Jayne.

"Ben?"

"I think so."

"Charlotte? Toby?"

"Yes."

"This way, all that Jarmyn saw was five long faces," Boff reminded them. "Your faces were long because you believed we hadn't cracked the code, and my face was long because I'd had to lie to you all. I'm sorry – but it worked perfectly, didn't it?"

Now that they'd got over the shock, they all agreed that it had. At last, they allowed their suppressed excitement to start taking over.

"Well?" said Ben. "What about the code, then?"

"What does it say?" said Charlotte.

"How did you do it?" said Jayne.

Boff stooped to the cubby-hole underneath the branch that ran at an angle through the tree-house and pulled out a rolled-up sheaf of papers. He crouched down with them and started to explain.

"I didn't really lie when I told Jarmyn that we hadn't kept any copies of his code. We've got our own copy in *Roject-pong Ubmarine song*, so we haven't really cheated at all. We haven't stolen the code from him. All it's made us do is crack Peter's code sooner than we might have done otherwise."

Boff spread the original message on the floor:

```
TNQBM HLVII ENQLF YUNEO SLVMQ RVKEG
TIVKG BBPOQ 24793 3TXGT YVVIZ SSHFX
```

"I don't need to tell you how many different ways we tried to solve it. I didn't read all of the code-breaking book, because I thought it was a waste of time. *If this code was meant to be unbreakable, I didn't think the writer would have taken it from a book that anyone could get hold of.* So I had to think of new ideas, hoping I'd hit on the same idea as his – or hers.

"In the end it was so simple, it was unbelievable. It was two o'clock this morning. I'd almost given up for the night, but I kept having new ideas, and I had to keep trying them out. And then—" Boff's voice quivered with excitement – "I had a *stupid* idea."

"What?"

"What was it?"

"I think my brain was going mad, trying to make me sleep, and coming up with funny dream-like things to give me hints that I was supposed to be in bed. I suddenly wondered what would happen if you added T and N together."

"If you add T and N you get a TAN," said Ben, grinning.

"Or a TIN," said Jayne.

"Or TEN," said Toby. "Or TON or TUN."

"That's not what I mean," said Boff. "Let's start with something simpler. What's A and B added together?"

They all thought in silence for a few seconds before Charlotte said, "I know. 'A' is the first letter in the alphabet, so that's one, and 'B' is the second, so that's two. 'A' plus 'B' means one plus two. That makes three."

"And what's the third letter in the alphabet?" Boff prompted her.

"C," said Charlotte.

"Good," said Boff. "So A plus B is C."

Charlotte latched on to the idea straight away.

"So T plus N would be . . ." she started counting on her fingers and muttering parts of the alphabet. "Well, T is the twentieth letter of the alphabet, and N is the fourteenth, so T plus N is twenty plus fourteen, which is thirty-four, so . . . Hang on, there aren't thirty-four letters in the alphabet!"

"But I want the answer as a letter," said Boff. "So what are you going to do?"

Charlotte frowned, and Toby jumped in before she had time to answer.

"Take away twenty-six!" he said. "It's like going round the alphabet again. Thirty-four minus twenty-six is eight, and the eighth letter is H. *Tong lus-pong ning is-ing heng*."

"Well done," said Boff.

"I don't get that bit," said Jayne. "Sorry to be thick."

"I'll make it simpler," said Boff. "A plus B is C – happy with that?"

"Yes," said Jayne firmly.

"So what's A plus C?"

"D," said Jayne promptly.

"A plus D?"

"E. This is getting easy now."

"A plus Y?"

"Z."

"So what's A plus Z?"

Jayne wrinkled her nose.

"Oh." A pause. "I want the next letter after Z, don't I?"

"You do. Which is?"

"'A', I suppose, if I'm allowed to go back to the beginning again."

"You are," said Boff. "And you're right. A plus Z is A. If you translate it into numbers, one plus twenty-six is twenty-seven. There isn't a twenty-seventh letter, so you take away twenty-six and you get one."

Jayne grinned.

"I understand!" she said.

"Brilliant!" said Boff. He looked round at them all, and the reflection of the windows of the tree-house rotated in his glasses like a camera panning the scene. "Now you know how to solve this code!"

Charlotte grabbed the sheet of paper that lay on the floor between them and peered at it closely, then wrote down all the letters of the alphabet with their numbers underneath:

| A | B | C | D | E | F | G | H | I | J | K | L | M |
|---|---|---|---|---|---|---|---|---|---|---|---|---|
| 1 | 2 | 3 | 4 | 5 | 6 | 7 | 8 | 9 | 10 | 11 | 12 | 13 |

| N | O | P | Q | R | S | T | U | V | W | X | Y | Z |
|---|---|---|---|---|---|---|---|---|---|---|---|---|
| 14 | 15 | 16 | 17 | 18 | 19 | 20 | 21 | 22 | 23 | 24 | 25 | 26 |

"First word TNQBM," she said. "T+N=H. We've already done that! N+Q. . . N is fourteen and Q is seventeen, that's thirty-one, minus twenty-six, that's five, which is E! N+Q=E!" Pleased with herself, Charlotte added the other letters, "Q+B=S; B+M=O. Hmmm. So far, I've got 'HESO'. I don't think any words begin with 'HESO'. . ."

"Carry on," said Boff. "Forget the words. They're just split up into fives to make it harder."

"So I carry on with HLVII?"

"Yes. Ignore the space. Add the H to the M from the first word."

"M+H=U; H+L=T; L+V=H; V+I=E; I+I=R. One more?"

"Two more. ENQLF and YUNEO."

"I+E=N; E+N=S; N+Q=E; Q+L=C; L+F=R; F+Y=E; Y+U=T; U+N=I; N+E=S; E+O=T."

"Stop there," said Boff. See what you've written."

Charlotte wrote the results neatly in a row.

HESO UTHER NSECR ETIST

"No," said Boff, "take away the spaces. Put in your own."

Charlotte felt her hand shaking as she closed the letters together.

HESOUTHERNSECRETISI

"Boff! Look! It's got the words 'SOUTHERN SECRET' in the middle! It's so exciting, I can hardly breathe!"

The others had craned closer as they saw the words forming under their noses, and Boff allowed himself another brief smile of satisfaction.

"Can you imagine how I felt when I saw those words coming?" he said. "I couldn't believe it. But then I couldn't figure why it said 'He southern secret' until I worked out an easier way of doing it. Then I realised how it worked."

Boff took another sheet of paper and wrote the first part of the code along the top line, without spaces, then wrote it again underneath, but pushed one place to the right. Then he drew a line underneath, and added each pair of letters together:

```
  T N Q B M H L V I I E N Q L F Y U N E O
  + T N Q B M H L V I I E N Q L F Y U N E +
  ---------------------------------------
  T H E S O U T H E R N S E C R E T I S T
```

Jayne read it out as Boff wrote each line. "The southern secret is t . . ."

```
  S L V M Q R V K E G T I V K G B B P O Q
+ O S L V M Q R V K E G T I V K G B B P O +
  ---------------------------------------
  H E H I D I N G P L A C E G R I D R E F
```

" . . . he hiding place grid ref . . . 247933 . . ."

```
  T X G T Y V V I Z S S H F X
  + T X G T Y V V I Z S S H F X
  ---------------------------
  T R E A S U R E I S L A N D
```

"Treasure Island! *The southern secret is the hiding place grid ref 247933 Treasure Island!* Boff, it's wonderful!"

"After I saw you this morning and went home to have a sleep I looked at the local Ordnance Survey map to see what was at that grid reference. There should be two letters on the front to fit it to the right map. Without the letters, you get the same reference every hundred kilometres. I looked up 247 and 933, but neither was on our local map. But that started me thinking. If it *was* just a map reference, people would be able to read that part of the message *without knowing the code*. I realised the reference would have to be in code, too. So I did the same thing with the numbers."

Boff wrote on the paper again.

"I put the six numbers down, then shifted them one to the right. I added up *each column separately* – subtracting any tens, like we subtracted twenty-sixes for the alphabet – and got . . ."

```
  2 4 7 9 3 3
+   2 4 7 9 3
-------------
  2 6 1 6 2 6
```

"Of course, I know it doesn't have to be a reference on *our* local map - it could be on another map altogether. But guess where map reference 261, 626 *is* on our local map?"

"We've no idea, Boff," said Charlotte. "Just show us."

Boff unfolded the map. They followed his fingers as they traced the co-ordinates 261 east and 626 north and came to a halt.

"Ghost Island!" said Toby.

"Ghost Island!" the others repeated.

"Yes," said Boff. "Ghost Island. *Treasure Island.* More than just a coincidence, don't you think?"

CHAPTER EIGHT

# *Ghost Island*

Ghost Island was a real island set in the middle of a lake about four miles from Naitabal territory. The lake was fed by a river, and drained by the same river at the other end. Ben traced its course with a stubby finger.

"Look!" he said. "It's our river!" He showed them Gray's Wood, then followed the river on its far side downstream. "We can go there on the raft!"

Suddenly there was tremendous excitement at the idea, and everyone wanted to get on the raft and start the exploration straight away.

"I think we should find out more about this Ghost Island first," said Jayne.

"I wonder who'd know about it?" said Charlotte.

"I know who'd know about it," said Ben, and they all said together, "Mr Elliott!"

Mr Elliott was the builder who had built their tree-house for them. He owned the Sea of Debris, and allowed them to use it as their headquarters. He also gave them free access to all his rubbish, which meant they were rarely short of materials for their projects. He'd been established in the district for forty years. He knew so many people and houses, it was almost certain he would know something about Ghost Island.

Mr Elliott worked all day and every weekend, and only came home when he needed to eat or sleep. Luckily, he came home most days for lunch.

As it was almost one o'clock now, the Naitabals decided to lock up the Naitabal hut and wait for Mr Elliott on his doorstep. They soon heard the rattle of his van a quarter of a mile away, its engine sounding like a box of loose spanners in a tumble dryer.

Nothing surprised Mr Elliott. He came towards them with his quick little steps as if they were there to greet him every day of the week. Clouds of dust flew off his overalls as he walked, spraying on to the ground in little white patches.

"Hello, mates," he said. "Come for a sandwich?"

By this time the Igmopong had spotted the Naitabals, and had sidled up to the hedge next door, making pathetic attempts to conceal themselves.

"May we speak to you inside, Mr Elliott?" said Charlotte in a loud voice, so the Igmopong could hear.

"Course you can, course you can."

He unlocked the door and led them through the hall into the kitchen. They were familiar with the inside of Mr Elliott's house. They'd looked after it for him once when he'd gone on an unexpected holiday. It was funny to think that all the rooms, apart from the kitchen, were packed with furniture so tight that it was almost impossible to open the doors to get into them.

"What can I do for you all?" he said.

"Have you heard of a place called Ghost Island?" said Charlotte, coming straight to the point.

"Ghost Island?" said Mr Elliott. "Coo! I'll say I have. I think everybody's heard of Ghost Island."

"We haven't, Mr Elliott."

"We'll soon put that right, then," said Mr Elliott. "To start with, Ghost Island is an island. But then again it's not, if you get my meaning."

"No, Mr Elliott, we don't."

Mr Elliott took out a loaf of bread and started cutting off thick slices with quick strokes of the bread knife. Toby fetched margarine, and he and Ben spread the bread as it came off the production line at prodigious speed.

"Ghost Island is the house, really."

"You mean there's a house on it!?"

"The house used to be called Ghost Eye, cos if you look at the map there's three islands in the lake. The shape of the lake looks like a ghost's head, and the islands look like its eyes and mouth. The other islands are just grassy humps, but Ghost Eye doesn't have any ground. The house just comes straight out of the water, like a castle does from a moat. Most people call it Ghost Island these days."

Mr Elliott had finished slicing bread and was now cutting a brick-size piece of cheese like a demon, flicking the pieces on to the waiting hunks of bread. Charlotte had put the kettle on for tea (extra strong for Mr Elliott), and Boff and Jayne were rounding up cups and spoons.

"Does anyone live there?" said Ben.

"Not now," said Mr Elliott. "It's been boarded up for twelve or thirteen years – no, near fourteen, it must be."

"But why? Why was it boarded up?"

"The man who owned it died, and no one's sorted out his will. All the furniture's still inside, but you can't get in. Some burglars tried once." Mr Elliott grunted with amusement.

"What happened?" said Jayne.

"Oh, they rowed their boat to the jetty, but that was as far as they got. Something frightened 'em so bad, they left the island in a big hurry. Their car – stolen, o' course – was found crashed not far away – with them still inside it, gibbering about seeing a ghost.

"Is it really haunted, then?"

"Haunted? I'll say! Coo! I'll say it's haunted. You wouldn't catch me working there again."

"Again?"

"You mean you actually went there?"

"What happened, Mr Elliott?"

"Well . . ."

Boff poured the tea, Jayne fetched plates, and the others handed round the big doorstep sandwiches as Mr Elliott told his story.

"The house is built on an island, see, but you can't really see the island any more," Mr Elliott began. "The house rises straight out of the water, like a castle more like, as I said, so you have to get there by boat. Well, the first thing I was told was that if you tried snooping round there in darkness, hands would come up out of the lake and tip your boat, then drag you under till you drowned."

Jayne shuddered.

"So I was in no mood for relaxin' when I went, I can tell you. I had to decorate two rooms on the first floor. Well, I was working a bit late one evening, and the owner was off somewhere in his boat, told me to stay until he got back, as he didn't want to leave the place open. It's got a drawbridge that comes down on to the jetty, see, and you can't shut it unless you know how. Anyway, I sees his boat coming far side of the lake, and I'm waiting on the jetty looking round when I sees this white figure walking across the top of the water and straight through the wall of the house . . ."

"Oh, Mr Elliott . . ."

"First and last ghost I've ever seen," Mr Elliott went on, "and I've no taste to see any more, neither. When I told the owner, he said it was the original path to the house in the eighteenth century. The person who owned it later, in 1810, diverted the river and flooded the place and made the lake. I had a look the next day. You can still see the marks where the old door's been bricked up. Straight through, she walked. On top of the water, and straight through the wall . . . No, I won't work there again, even if they pay me double."

The scary look in Mr Elliott's eyes disappeared, and he turned to the Naitabals.

"You're not thinkin' o' goin' there, are you?"

"Well . . ."

"I wouldn't if I were you, but – well, that's your decision mates. Just be careful, that's all. It's a private lake, mind, so you shouldn't really go there, strictly legal, like. But then, kids on a river . . . You never know where you might end up, do you?"

Mr Elliott finished his lunch with a twinkle in his eye, and rushed off to work again.

"Don't bother about clearing up," he said as he disappeared through the front door, "if you don't want to. I'll do it with the rest when I get back tonight."

"Thanks, Mr Elliott! Bye!"

They heard the cacophony of sound as his van started up, and listened until it rattled into the distance.

"Let's clear up, anyway," said Toby. "For a surprise."

"Yes!" said Charlotte. "Then . . . Ghost Island!"

"We'll need life-jackets," said Ben when they were back in the Naitabal tree-house, away from the flapping ears of the Igmopong.

"I haven't got one," said Toby.

"Nor me," said Jayne.

"It's lucky my family's got three, then," said Charlotte.

"We've got three, as well," said Boff, "so that's enough for all of us – as long as they fit."

"We'll need food," said Ben.

"It's your turn to bring food," said Charlotte. "I vote you and Toby to bring the food."

"Okay. And we'll need torches, ropes . . ."

"Standard Naitabal equipment," said Jayne. "In other words, Naitabal battledress."

"I don't think we need to be drastic," said Boff. "All we can do without breaking the law is to go and look at the place. What we can do after that depends on what we see. We certainly can't go breaking and entering."

"But it's abandoned," said Toby. "It doesn't matter if we go inside. How can we solve the puzzle or find the treasure if we don't?"

"It's not abandoned," said Ben, reluctantly agreeing with Boff. There was nothing Ben wanted more than to get inside the house somehow, but he sensed where to draw the line. "It's just been boarded up for fourteen years."

"Fourteen years!" said Charlotte suddenly. "I've just realised!"

"What?"

"The house has been boarded up for nearly fourteen years, and it's nearly fourteen years since that letter was sent to Peter's mother! Don't you remember – it's got the date on the envelope, and Peter is thirteen years old! That *proves* the house has got something to do with it!"

"It could just be a coincidence," said Boff, then added after a moment's thought, "But I doubt it," and grinned.

"Is there anything else we'll need?" asked Jayne.

"A gun," said Toby, grinning. "And grappling hooks to scale the walls, and . . ."

"Thank you for that useful contribution, Toby," said Charlotte. "Are you returning to planet earth today? Any serious suggestions?"

"Perhaps a camera," suggested Jayne. "It might be a good idea to take photos from each angle so we can study them back here."

"Good one," said Charlotte. "Any others?"

"That's about it," said Ben. "Let's just go and have a look."

Their excitement mounted as they took everything they needed from the Naitabal hut, locked it against illegal occupation by the Igmopong, and descended to the Sea of Debris. They carried the raft into Boff's front garden, fetched provisions and the other essentials they'd discussed, including Boff and Charlotte's life-jackets. At the same time they each asked their parents' permission for the trip, and gave assurances that they would be back well before dark.

All the while, they sensed the Igmopong watching from the safety of Cedric's front garden. The sound of regular arguments and shaking shrubbery always gave them away.

"Where do you think they're taking the raft?" said Doris from inside the hedge.

"How am I supposed to know?" said Cedric. "I'm not a mind reader."

"You're not much of a mind *user*, either," retorted Doris, stung by Cedric's unhelpful answer.

"What's that supposed to mean?"

"Well, if you can't think of one place they might be going with their raft, it doesn't say much for your brain, does it?"

"Can you think of somewhere, then?"

As it happened, Doris had spent the previous half hour poring over a map of the local area. It seemed logical, as the Naitabals built their first raft near the river, that they would be sailing it *on* the river. She had traced its meandering course and was intrigued to discover that it ran into a large lake. She was even more intrigued to find that the lake had islands in the middle.

She looked belligerently into Cedric's face where his bulging eyes were challenging her.

"Ghost Island," she said.

A man sat in his car at the end of Brunswick Road, looking towards the houses opposite the entrance to the wood. He had a shock of dark, untidy hair, and a full bushy beard and moustache like a squirrel's nest, with his mouth hidden behind the entrance. He was wearing black jeans and a red tartan shirt, and he was looking through binoculars.

He sat patiently, hour after hour, watching and waiting. Now that he was retired, he had plenty of time to watch, and listen, and wait. Sometimes there was a movement of children in the gardens, and he would raise his binoculars to take a closer look.

After only a few hours of waiting and watching from his car, he had his first reward. He saw a group of children carrying a raft across the road and into the woods. There was only one place they could be going with a raft, he thought. He took out his local map and studied it. His finger traced its way through the woods to the river, then along the line of the river.

"I wonder?" he said aloud to himself, and smiled.

The river carried on after the lake, but the man's finger didn't. It stopped at Ghost Island.

The most difficult part of the Naitabals' journey to Ghost Island was carrying the raft through Gray's Wood. By the time it had been loaded with equipment and provisions it was too heavy to carry any distance, so it was unloaded again, then carried by four of them while Toby stayed behind and guarded the luggage. It was another half an hour before Jayne and Charlotte reappeared and helped Toby on the final trek with the cargo.

Even as they disappeared into the woods, they heard car doors slamming and glimpsed Cedric's father's car pulling away from the kerb and crawling up the road.

Ben and Boff were waiting on the river bank with the raft poised on the edge. They all loaded the provisions.

Jayne had brought a plastic bottle to launch it with, which she filled with water from the river. She screwed on the top, then held it up on a string. She gave the loose end of the string to Toby, who held it up high above the raft.

Jayne stepped back as far as the string would allow, said, "I name this ship *Naitabal II.* God bless her and all who sail in her," and swung the bottle hard. It hit the sharp corner of the plank on the stern, and burst its contents on to the bank.

Then, with loving care, the Naitabals lowered *Naitabal II* into the river.

It floated beautifully. As each of them stepped on, first Charlotte and Ben in the for'ard seats, then Jayne at the tiller, it sank lower and lower. They began to wonder if twelve plastic barrels were enough. But as Toby and Boff climbed into the chairs astern, it settled to the perfect height, with the seats of the rowing chairs a few centimetres above the level of the water. Then Charlotte and Boff pushed off with their oars.

Their journey had begun.

They paddled to the middle of the river, legs stretched out in front to gain compass on the rungs of the ladders, enjoying the gentle bounce and the tug of the current. It was an exhilarating feeling as the grassy banks and trees started to slip by. The first few fields and banks were half-familiar, explored on foot in times past, but soon their surroundings became new and strange and exciting. Now there were trees hanging low over the water, now a gentle curve, now a bank of sandy soil eroded and fallen in, now horses grazing against a nearby fence, now two ducks swerving to avoid the strange craft as it made its stately progress downstream.

After about a mile they came to a low bridge with five arches. As they approached, they calculated that they could get through, but it was a tight squeeze. All four rowers had to duck down in their chairs to get under it, and be ready to fend off with their oars as the stronger current pulled them through the narrow gap. They came through safely and took the opportunity to change positions and steersman and for Jayne to take her turn at paddling.

The current and their efforts carried them steadily onward. After another two miles, they rounded yet another left hand sweep of the river. Way ahead, the bank was receding as the expanse of water widened, and they could see a grassy hump out in the middle in the distance. As they continued to swing to the left, the lake suddenly opened up in front of them. It was a wonderful sight, and they all stopped paddling.

"Look!" said Jayne.

They couldn't help looking. Ahead of them, a third of the way across the big lake, a sinister house rose straight out of the water. Its walls climbed vertically with no visible land to support them, and its windows were blindfolded with wooden boards.

"Ghost Island!" Toby whispered.

## CHAPTER NINE

# *Tranded-song*

Cedric Morgan and the other Igmopong waited until the figures of Toby, Jayne and Charlotte merged in with the trees of Gray's Wood, then sprang into action.

"They've all gone!" Cedric squealed. "Come on!"

He ran into his house and found his father in the sitting-room.

"Dad! Hey, Dad! Can we go now?"

Mr Morgan was a weedy, henpecked little man with a smoker's cough who always reacted to the sound of a command. It didn't matter who gave the command, he just obeyed it. As soon as he heard the voice – Cedric's voice, as it happened – he pulled himself out of his chair and obediently followed to the car. The back seats were already stuffed with life-jackets, picnic baskets, paddles and assorted Igmopong, and it only remained for Mr Morgan to work the controls and deliver them to their destination. He never argued and he only asked those questions needed to complete his task. He obeyed.

"Where are we going?" he said, breaking into a coughing fit.

"Just go up the road and turn left, and I'll show you," said Cedric. "It's where I showed you on the map. Where our raft is, remember?"

"Oh, yes, I remember."

Before the car drove off, Mrs Morgan came rushing out of the house and forced big wet kisses on Cedric and Doris.

"Now be careful, my darlings," she said, looking worried. "The river can be very dangerous, but I know you'll be careful."

"Yes, Mum," said Cedric, wiping his kiss off.

"And come back before dark."

"Yes, Mum," said Doris, wiping hers off.

"And telephone as soon as you're ready to be collected."

"Yes, Mum."

"And if you get wet, come *straight* home."

"Yes, Mum," said Cedric irritably, then hastily commanded, "You can go now, Dad!"

Mr Morgan started the engine, Mrs Morgan planted two more big kisses by stretching Cedric and Doris's heads out of the car window, and then they were off, wiping their cheeks again.

After a ten minute journey through winding country lanes they arrived at the house near the river where their stolen raft was grounded out of sight. Five minutes after Mr Morgan had gone back home, they had donned their life-jackets and finished loading the raft. Then they dragged it as near to the river as possible without being visible to passing Naitabals.

They lay in wait in some thick undergrowth near the water's edge.

"Now listen," said Cedric. "We've got to keep *really quiet*. Otherwise those stupid Naitabals will see us."

"If we've got to keep really quiet," said Doris, "how come you're talking already?"

"Because I'm giving instructions, that's why," said Cedric, annoyed.

"And don't you mean if we don't keep really quiet, the Naitabals will *hear* us? You said 'see us'?"

"No, I don't, and stop arguing, and stop talking. If we carry on shouting and arguing they'll see *and* hear us. We mustn't let them know we're here, not ever. Once they know where we've hidden their – our – raft, we're sunk."

"Sunk," said Doris, lowering her voice. "Was that meant to be a joke?"

"Only speak," said Cedric through clenched teeth, "if I say so. Unless it's really urgent, then you can speak in a whisper. And don't move unless I say so. Got it?"

"Are we allowed to *breathe*?" said Doris, who couldn't resist a final fling of sarcasm.

"Preferably not," said Cedric. "Just shut up, okay?"

By some miraculous means, the Igmopong managed to remain hidden and silent for the thirty minutes it took for their quarry – the Naitabals – to pass by on the river just below the ridge where they were hiding.

When they had gone, Cedric tapped his watch and whispered.

"We'll give them another three minutes, then we'll follow them."

"It's wonderful!" said Jayne.

The Naitabals were all transfixed. The house on Ghost Island was just like a castle, its majestic castellated walls silhouetted against the sky, towering above the lake. Thick, round wooden posts stuck up out of the water a few metres from the house, like giant hippo teeth. They must once have been the trunks of big trees, and enclosed the whole house as far as their eyes could see. Further down the lake, they glimpsed the grassy knolls of two more islands, the mouth and second eye of the ghost that Mr Elliott had described.

Instinctively, they started pushing on their oars again, propelling themselves nearer and nearer to the building, as if in a dream.

They swung slightly to one side, watching as it loomed closer and closer, until another sheer wall came into view.

"There's a bricked-up door in that one!" said Charlotte. "Look!"

They looked. Sure enough, almost at the level of the water, they could see the outline of where a door had been. They could see its stone lintel and wooden frame, but now just stones and mortar where the door had once stood.

"I bet that's the door where Mr Elliott saw the ghost walk through," said Ben.

They all gazed at it in silence, feeling a mixture of excitement, intrigue and fear.

"I think I'd die if she walked across the water now," said Jayne. "But I'd love to see a real ghost – just once."

"It would be just once if you died straight after it," said Toby, and the others laughed. Except Boff, who was at the prow of the raft now, looking at the house through binoculars.

As they continued their circular tour, the jetty came into view. It was opposite the far side of the house, and it stood on four even bigger wooden pillars, rising straight out of the water to a height of almost a metre. Behind it, on the sheer wall of the house, was the only visible entrance – a small drawbridge. It rose vertically from its hinges at the same level as the jetty, about four metres high and two metres wide, and was shut firmly against the face of the building. A large red sign hung in its middle, with big letters saying,

PRIVATE. KEEP OFF

TRESPASSERS WILL BE PROSECUTED

"The drawbridge comes down on to the jetty," said Ben.

"That's the only place to land," said Jayne.

"What do you think all the other posts are for?" said Toby. "Look. They go right round the house."

"Perhaps they're to stop boats bumping into the house. It must be really annoying to be sitting down to dinner and having someone rowing past and looking through your windows."

"It must help stop burglars, then," said Charlotte. "If you can't get a boat right up to the house, you can't break in –

not very easily, anyway."

"And if they get too close, the ghost gets them," said Toby, with relish.

They manoeuvred the raft alongside the little jetty, and tied it to one of the posts. They all climbed out and stood on the wooden boards, staring up at the blanked-out windows and the drawbridge that stood vertically in front of them.

"Those posts are near enough together to stop even a rowing boat getting in between them," said Charlotte, studying them more closely.

"Yes," said Ben. "And they're near enough together for something else as well . . ."

"What?"

Ben showed them. He stood at the side of the jetty and took a long stride towards the top of the first post.

"Ben!"

The top was wide and flat, and he found he could stand on it comfortably with both feet.

"It's safe enough," he said.

"Ben – it's dangerous."

"We've got life-jackets on. Come on, let's go right round." Ben demonstrated by stepping on to the next post, then the next. "You're not all scared, are you?"

Charlotte couldn't let Ben get away with a challenge like that. She had to admit to herself it did seem safe enough, as long as it wasn't done in too much of a rush. She stepped on to the first post, and Toby followed, then Jayne. They enjoyed the novelty of hopping from post to post and getting a closer – and higher – view of the house than if they were going round in the raft. Boff only joined them when he realised that it was one way that he might get a better look at some parts of the building.

They moved slowly along the first side until Ben stopped and pointed up at one of the windows. The others caught up until all five of them were standing on five consecutive posts.

"That window's been bricked up," said Ben, "not just boarded up."

They stood for a few minutes absorbing every detail, even though there wasn't much to see, then slowly moved on. They examined every side of the house, but there was little else they could do. All the windows were boarded up, and the only visible door was bricked up. It looked as though the drawbridge was the only possible entrance.

"I don't understand how the owner can get in," said Toby, "if you can't even reach the walls by boat. I mean, if he came back tomorrow, how would he open the drawbridge?"

"It could be operated like one of those automatic garage doors," said Boff. "He'd have an infra-red or an ultrasound control. He'd arrive at the jetty, point the control, and bring the drawbridge down. Easy."

They were halfway round by now, and it was only when they had started on the third side and the little jetty came into view again, that Jayne noticed something.

"That's odd."

"What?"

"I thought we tied the raft to the jetty? I can't see it from here."

The others stopped at the posts they were on and Ben, who was in front, hopped forward a few more to get a better angle of view.

"Jayne's right!" he called. "The raft has gone!"

"Gone? It can't have!"

"We tied it really well," said Toby. "I did one end and Jayne did the other."

"Yes. We definitely tied it to the posts."

Ben had continued post-stepping faster now, and the others were trying to catch up.

"Can you see it drifting anywhere?" said Boff. He was in the worst position at the back of the procession, and there was real anxiety in his voice. "One of us will have to swim after it."

"There's no sign of it," said Ben and Charlotte together.

"We can't see it *anywhere*," said Jayne.

By the time they had all arrived safely back on the jetty, the situation was perfectly obvious to all of them. They could all see for themselves. The surface of the lake was flat and calm and empty, and the raft had completely disappeared without trace.

As soon as their three minutes were up, the Igmopong sprang into action and launched their raft. They'd had some practice now, and managed to get under way without any mishaps.

Somehow, they paddled quietly down the river without a single word being spoken. Somehow, they slowed at every bend while Cedric leaned out as far as he dared and made sure the Naitabals were still out of sight. Somehow, they completed the entire journey and reached the lake without being seen or heard. The first words were spoken by Cedric in an excited whisper. He was craning his neck again to see if the coast was clear across the lake.

"There's a house in the middle of the lake!" he said. "I can see the Naitabals on their raft!"

"I told you," hissed Doris. "Ghost Island."

He instructed his oarsmen to go back a bit. They pulled the raft against the bank where Cedric could still see by leaning out sideways.

"They're going round the other side of the house!" he continued his commentary. "Get ready to paddle when I say 'Now!', and remember to do it quietly!"

They waited at the inside of the bend until Cedric gave the signal, then Doris and Amanda heaved on the paddles while Cedric waved his hands to show Andy which way to steer with their rudimentary rudder. Owing more to luck than skill, the raft slid away from the bank.

As they emerged on to the lake, *Naitabal II* was already hidden behind the house, and the Igmopong were able to row all the way to the line of posts on the opposite side. Once there, Cedric made them all lie flat so that they and the raft were below the level of the posts. They discovered that they could propel the raft by holding the posts and pulling themselves along, with Doris keeping a look-out on the outer edge.

For once, incredible luck was on the Igmopong's side. They had emerged on to the lake at the moment when the Naitabals were disappearing behind Ghost Island. Not only that, but the Naitabals had stayed at the front of the house by the drawbridge for as long as it took the Igmopong to row quietly across to the back. And now, Cedric had to choose which way to start going round the house, and the right moment to do it.

He'd been lucky again. Even as the Naitabals started their anti-clockwise post-hopping tour, so the Igmopong slid along on the opposite side until they rounded the corner and reached the unguarded Naitabal raft, still unseen.

None of them could believe their luck could hold so long.

"Untie their ropes!" hissed Cedric.

Still, there were no arguments. Even the Igmopong sensed the coming triumph. None of them knew where the Naitabals had gone – in fact is seemed like a magic trick – but none of them had time to care. Here was the Naitabals' raft, and here was their chance to take it.

They freed the ropes in a few seconds, tied one of them to Andy's chair at the back, then started paddling slowly forward. They still didn't know it, but they were exactly opposite the Naitabals, still hidden by the house between them. They continued their anti-clockwise circumnavigation of the house and headed back towards the safety of the mouth of the river.

They stopped rowing and looked back at Ghost Island.

"It can't have disappeared," cried Jayne, "it can't!"
"It looks pretty disappeared to me," said Toby.
"And me," said Charlotte. "But it just isn't possible, is it?"
They all scanned the surface of the water and the distant banks. Ben peered into the depths to see if it had disobeyed the laws of physics and sunk. The only parts of the lake and banks they couldn't see were where Ghost Island loomed behind them, blocking their view of the mouth of the river.
"Ben!" said Boff suddenly.
"What?"
"Go round on the posts again, that way" – he pointed – "and I'll go this way. Quick!"
The others cottoned on to the idea. Boff and Charlotte went back the way they had come, while Ben, followed by Jayne and Toby, went round in the original direction. Even before they met up on the far side, and faced the entrance to the river to the north, they saw how the magic had been done.
Their dismayed silence was broken by a hoot of laughter from Cedric in the distance. The sound of Doris's voice reached them, clear and sharp as it echoed across the expanse of dark water.
"We've got *two* rafts now!" it said.
It was followed by Cedric's.
"And you're *stranded*!"

It wasn't just the raft that had gone. All their provisions, their torches, their spare ropes – everything except the Naitabal battledress they stood up in.
"How could we let them do it!" screamed Charlotte, disgusted with herself more than with the Igmopong. "Why didn't we leave someone to guard the raft?"
"Because we didn't even think they might have been

behind us," said Ben. "We always see them if they are. You know what it's like when they're following us. They *always* make a noise and give themselves away."

"How did they do it, then?" said Jayne.

"Sheer luck, as usual," said Toby. "They must have crossed the lake when we were on the jetty, and crept round the other way when we were going round on the posts."

"It's a miracle they didn't make any noise," said Charlotte. "They're usually like a tree full of monkeys."

"Boff!" said Jayne suddenly. "What about the secret code?"

"It's okay, thank goodness. It's in my pocket. There's no chance they'll see that."

They watched for another minute as the jeering Igmopong disappeared with the two rafts, round the curve and up the river, out of sight.

"What do we do now?" said Charlotte.

"Go back to the jetty to start with," said Boff. "It'll be a lot more comfortable than trying to balance on these posts. And be careful. They're slippery."

They all turned back towards the little jetty. They picked their way carefully, stepping from post to post, then stood in a huddle to discuss the unexpected crisis.

"Perhaps someone will see us from the shore," said Jayne, hopefully.

"It's not very likely," said Charlotte. "I think this lake is private, like the house. It belongs to whoever owns Ghost Island. And if the house has been deserted for nearly fourteen years, I don't see why anyone should happen to be strolling on the shore, do you?"

"Unless it's someone like us," said Toby. "Trespassing." He pointed. Sure enough, there were signs around the lake, scattered at intervals. "I bet they say, 'Trespassers Will Be Prosecuted'," he added.

"Don't, Toby," said Jayne. "It feels bad enough being

marooned here in the first place, without worrying about being trespassers and sitting ducks if anyone comes to arrest us."

"So how do we get out of his one?" said Charlotte.

"One of us will have to swim for it," said Toby.

They all looked at Ben, and Ben grinned.

"I'll swim to the shore," he said. "I don't mind."

Boff had been thinking.

"I think the Igmopong will come back," he said.

"Never!" said Toby. "Not now they've got us stranded."

"Yes they will," said Boff firmly. "Half their pleasure comes from taunting us, and they can't taunt us when they're miles away up the river."

"What do you think they'll do, then?" said Jayne.

"When their brains have woken up, they'll realise they can bargain with us – blackmail, if you like."

"I can guess what they'll want," groaned Charlotte, and the others chanted together, "*A week in our tree-house!*"

"Well, they're not going to get it," said Ben. "I'd much rather swim and get help than let that rabble into our tree-house, even for an hour."

"It's a long way to shore, Ben," said Charlotte, worried. "Further than it looks."

"It's only a few hundred metres," said Ben. "I've done that loads of times. It's only twelve lengths."

"In a nice warm swimming pool," Charlotte reminded him, "with lifeguards all round and a nice rail to grab hold of if you swallow some water."

"I've got a life-jacket."

"It's the cold that might be the problem," said Jayne, sounding concerned. "It's autumn. You'll get hypothermia if you don't find help quickly enough."

"We might all freeze to death anyway," retorted Ben, "stuck out here all night."

"I think swimming for help is a last resort," said Boff.

"We'll wait a bit for the Igmopong to come back. They're bound to."

"Perhaps we can jump their raft—" said Toby.

"*Our* raft," corrected Jayne.

"Our *rafts*," corrected Charlotte.

" – And leave the Igmopong on Ghost Island," Toby went on. "Then we could tell their parents we'd seen them here and let *them* sort it out."

"And get into trouble for stealing 'their' raft," said Charlotte. "You know what Cedric's like. He'd kick up a *huge* fuss if we left *him* stranded."

"He always reverts to babyhood when he's in trouble," said Jayne, "screaming and kicking and calling for his mother."

"We need a plan of action," said Ben, "that's what we need."

"I don't see what we can do," said Charlotte, "stuck in the middle of a lake with no means of escape."

"It's not as bad as that," said Ben. "We've got out of worse situations than this."

Jayne looked up at the house – Ghost Eye – towering above them only a few metres away, yet completely out of reach.

"It's *maddening*," she said. "It's so close, and yet there's no way we can even *look* inside, let alone *get* inside."

"I can't see how we can get any further with the coded message now," said Toby.

"What do you mean?" said Jayne.

"Well – how can we explore the secret of Ghost Island and find the treasure, or the stolen goods, or the whatever-it-is? We can't even look in through a window, or touch the front door. Let's face it. This is as close as we're ever going to get."

"If we had grappling irons and ropes," said Ben, going off on one of his flights of fantasy, "we could scale the walls and climb in through a skylight in the roof . . . We could—"

"And if we had a helicopter . . ." said Charlotte. "That's just it – we haven't, so we can't."

Ben was pointing up high and was about to say something else when Jayne suddenly grabbed his arm to silence him.

"Listen!" she hissed.

They all listened. The only sounds that came to them were the very gentle lapping of water against the wooden posts and the wall of the house, and a faint breath of wind.

"What was it?" whispered Charlotte.

"Listen!" said Jayne again.

Again they listened. This time they all heard what Jayne had heard. It was a sound that they least expected to hear. At the same time it was a sound that filled their hearts with a strange feeling of dread and foreboding.

It came from behind the boarded windows of the house on Ghost Island. It was the unmistakable sound of someone crying.

## CHAPTER TEN

# *Ost-gheng*

Cedric Morgan and the Igmopong stopped rowing as soon as they entered the mouth of the river. Before the gentle current carried them back out into the lake again, they took up their paddles hastily and pulled themselves towards a low bank on the far side where they could land the rafts and enjoy their triumph. They unpacked their food and started eating.

"Did you see the looks on their faces . . .?" said Andy, sniggering.

"No!" snapped Doris. "They were too far away, remember?"

Andy stopped sniggering.

"Oh, yeah."

"But we could *imagine* the looks on their faces," said Amanda, supporting her brother. "They just stood there on those posts looking sick, didn't they?"

"Yeah," said Andy, sniggering again.

"They'll *never* get out of that one," said Cedric. "There's no one in that house – did you know? Doris asked our mum. She says it's been boarded up for years, so there won't be anyone in *there* to rescue them."

"I wonder how much they'd give us to get their raft back," said Doris, calculating.

"We could get a week in their tree-house!" said Amanda.

The others liked the idea, but their discussion was interrupted by the sight of a rowing boat coming downstream at a good speed. As soon as the rower saw them he seemed to hesitate for a second, but then had a closer look and turned the prow of his boat straight towards them.

There was only one man in the boat, and as he approached they could see his features more clearly. He had an untidy shock of dark hair, bushy eyebrows and a very bushy beard. He was wearing a bright red tartan shirt and black jeans.

"Ahoy, there!" he called in a Scottish accent.

The Igmopong liked the sound of him, and relaxed.

"Hello," said Cedric. "We're pirates, so you'd better not come too close."

"You'll slit ma throat, will you?" said the man.

His boat nudged into the sandy soil at the edge of the river, and he shipped his oars. The current wasn't strong enough to take his boat away, so it stayed there without needing to be tied up.

"You've been having fun, by the looks of it," the man went on. "I see you've two rafts. Didn't I see you up the river a while back with only the one?"

"I already told you," said Cedric, trying to look menacing, "we're pirates. We've just captured a ship."

"Where are the crew?"

"We killed them all," said Cedric, unabashed.

"We slit their throats," said Doris.

"And cut off their arms and legs," said Amanda.

"And then made them walk the plank," said Andy.

The other three turned their heads to glare at Andy, and the man laughed.

"Was that *after* you'd cut off their arms and legs?" he said. "My, you're a bloodthirsty lot."

"Yes," repeated Cedric. "We're pirates."

"Well, it's a pity you've dispensed with the crew of the other ship, because I wanted to have a word with them."

"How much treasure will you give us," said Doris promptly, sensing a deal, "if we tell you where we left their bodies?"

"How about a crisp doubloon?" said the man, taking a very

un-gold twenty pound note from his back pocket.

"That'll do," said Doris, leaning across and snatching it. "We left their bodies on the jetty – by the house on the lake. They've probably been eaten by the gulls by now," she added, as a warning.

"How long ago?"

"Fifteen minutes."

The man smiled, pushed his boat away from the bank, and glided backwards into the stream. He took up his oars again and pulled downstream towards the bend and the lake.

The man congratulated himself as he rowed away from the pirates. There was no doubt now where the other children had been heading. It had taken over half an hour for him to find someone with a rowing boat, and he'd thought his chances of catching up with them were slim. But his luck had held. Ghost Island! The very house that had once been owned by Reg Masters. Reg Masters, the man who had written the secret code. Reg Masters, the man who had died of a heart attack in a police cell the day after his arrest.

It could mean only one thing: in spite of the thorough search that was carried out by the police all those years ago, the stuff was hidden in Ghost Island after all.

The current and his strong rowing had already carried him out on to the lake, but the house itself hid the jetty from his line of sight. He chose the shortest route and circled the island until the wooden planks of the jetty came into view.

He stopped rowing.

The house stood blank and boarded up, blind and deaf to everything around it. It told him nothing. All he could see was that the posts around the house, and the jetty, were completely empty. There were no stranded children in sight, and no bodies.

Those scheming pirates had taken his money and told him a pack of lies.

*

"It's – it's someone *crying*," said Charlotte. "Listen!"

They listened, and the sound came again – a pitiful sobbing. There was nowhere else it could have come from except from inside the house. They were all dumbfounded, and it took fully a minute before Charlotte found the courage to speak again.

"Is there someone in there?" she called. "Are you hurt?"

The crying stopped. Now there was a rumbling, grating noise, deep in the lake, so it seemed. They could feel its vibration through the wooden boards at their feet, shaking their legs, as if their legs weren't shaking enough already. On the surface of the water, tiny patterns of ripples fanned out under the jetty.

"What is it?" said Jayne. "I think I'm scared!"

"No wonder people say the house is haunted," said Boff at last.

"It *is* haunted," said Jayne, miserably. "I don't like it! I wish we could get away!"

Even as Jayne spoke, her words turned into a stifled scream. Her face went deathly white, and her limp hand pointed round the side of the house. She couldn't speak any more, and the others followed the direction of her quivering arm.

A figure in a long, white dress and a white hood was standing on top of the water between two of the wooden posts. Even as they watched, the apparition walked slowly across the empty surface of the water that separated the posts and the house, and disappeared from view towards the wall.

The low grumble came again, sending unsettling vibrations through their feet. Jayne was shaking too much to move. Charlotte and Ben, who recovered the quickest, squeezed past her. They clambered from post to post, trying to see round the corner of the house, following the trail of the ghost, trying to see if it was still there on the water.

Charlotte was in front, and turned her pallid face to the others.

"It's disappeared!" she said, and now she was shaking badly, too. As she stepped back to the safety of the jetty, Ben had to steady her in case she shook herself into the water.

Boff and Toby hadn't moved. They were still standing, open-mouthed, rooted to the planks.

"It's disappeared!" Charlotte howled again. "It's gone through the wall where they bricked up the door!"

"It's the same ghost Mr Elliott saw," said Ben, who was first to recover from the shock. He quickly set out across the posts again, followed by Boff. They reached the place where they'd seen the figure, then looked down into the water.

"There's nowhere to stand between the posts," said Ben, looking closely. "And nowhere to walk across, either." To prove his point, he lowered himself on one leg and dangled his other foot deep in the water opposite the bricked-up door.

The others followed on to the posts again, watching and waiting, almost expecting a repeat performance from the ghost. But no ghost appeared.

They wondered what to do next. It wasn't every day they saw a ghost, and it certainly wasn't every day they were trapped on an island with one.

"We've really seen the ghost of Ghost Island!" said Jayne, who had recovered from her first fright, and was beginning to enjoy the experience – now that it was over.

"You didn't die," said Toby, complaining.

"What do you mean?"

"You said you'd die if you saw the ghost, and you didn't. Well, not yet, anyway. Perhaps you'll die a bit later."

"If I do, I'll haunt *you* for ever!" said Jayne.

"I think that was the oddest thing I've ever seen in my life," said Boff.

"And me," said Ben.

"Me, too," said Charlotte. She laughed. "I want to see it again now – now that I've got over the shock."

There was another shock to come – but it wasn't a ghost. They had all turned to retrace their steps to the jetty, when there was a flurry of arms and legs, a half-cut-off yell, a bump, and a huge splash. Toby had missed his footing on one of the slippery posts and fallen into the water. He bobbed to the surface in his life-jacket the right way up, and swam for the jetty. The others hurried across the posts to help him.

"Are you okay, Toby?"

"How did you manage that?"

"Did you hurt yourself?"

By the time they had helped him out of the water he was already shivering, and it was evident that he had badly knocked his shin. He rolled up the soaking leg of his jeans and they could see the nasty graze which was beginning to ooze blood.

"It only hurts a bit," said Toby. "I think the cold water's made it go numb."

"We're really in trouble now," said Charlotte. "Unless Toby gets dry pretty quickly, he's going to get really cold."

"This is what worried me about swimming for it," said Boff. He threw worried glances at Toby's dripping, shivering body.

They had hardly had time to regain their breath when there was another shaking, grinding hum accompanied by a high pitched whine. It seemed to fill the air around them, and it was difficult to say exactly where it came from. They soon found out.

"Oh dear!" Jayne blurted out. "I've changed my mind! I don't think I want to see the ghost again!"

They all looked up at the house, trying to pinpoint the sound, when there followed yet another surprising event. The massive drawbridge suddenly rumbled and creaked and started lurching slowly down towards them on monstrous chains.

## CHAPTER ELEVEN

# *Disappearing Act*

The lowering of the drawbridge was the very last thing the Naitabals had expected.

They stood ready to leap on to the posts again if the drawbridge threatened to squash them, but it came to rest on a small recess behind the jetty, so that both floors were level. The house gaped at them, opened up like Aladdin's cave.

Silence.

The Naitabals stood staring at the house and each other. The open drawbridge had exposed an oak front door, which was open, and two more windows, which were not boarded up. Through the windows and the door they could see dim lights glowing inside the house.

"W-what d-do w-we d-do n-now?" whispered Toby, shivering violently.

"I don't know about the rest of you," said Ben, "but I think we should get Toby inside and get him dry. I'm going in to check it out."

"So am I," said Charlotte.

"Some of us should stay out here," said Jayne anxiously. "Just in case anything goes wrong."

"I'll go in with Toby," said Ben. "If anything goes wrong, the rest of you can swim and get help."

"I'll come with you," said Charlotte.

"Okay."

"I want to come as well," said Jayne, changing her mind. "I don't think I can bear to be left out here with that ghost."

It was beginning to feel decidedly chilly in the cool air on the lake, even for those with dry clothes on, and a wind was getting up. In the end, even though it meant taking a bigger risk than they would have liked, it seemed most important to get Toby out of the wind as quickly as possible. There were no volunteers for staying outside and freezing to death in the open.

"Come on, then," said Boff. "We're in this together. Let's all go in."

Their minds made up, they walked slowly across the drawbridge and in through the front door. As soon as they were inside the spacious hall the humming, vibrating sound began again and the drawbridge closed majestically behind them. Jayne started to turn as if she'd changed her mind again, but Ben gripped her arm.

"Come on," he said. "We'll be all right." He dropped his voice to a comforting whisper. "*This is where we wanted to be. Inside Ghost Island at last.*"

The man rowed twice more around Ghost Island. There was definitely no sign of children on the jetty, and there was no sign of anyone on the banks of the lake. If they had been left there only fifteen minutes ago, it was impossible. They couldn't have escaped so quickly without trace. The bunch of pirates must have told him even less of the truth than he'd thought.

Looking grim, he hauled on his oars once more and headed towards the mouth of the river again.

"We're stupid if we just take their raft," said Doris. "What are we going to do with it if we're not going to make them bargain for it?"

Cedric giggled.

"We've left them stranded, that's what we've done."

"So one of them'll swim to the shore and get help, and then they'll be rescued, and then they'll come and get us. Good plan," said Doris bitterly.

Cedric's smile faded.

"Do you think we should take it back, then, now that they've had a fright?"

"Not just take it back . . ." said Doris, prompting him.

"What, then?"

"Can't you see? *Trade it in.* Trade it in for a few days in their tree-house."

"And what if they don't want to?"

"We'll just let their raft drift away, and they can swim for it. Then if anyone says anything we can say they didn't tie it up properly and it was their own fault and they're just trying to blame things on us. Then we won't get into trouble."

"Okay," said Cedric, feeling too tired from rowing to argue. "Let's do that, then."

They finished the last few bites of food and drink, tidied up their raft, and pushed off again into the welcoming current. As soon as they had rounded the curve that brought Ghost Island back into view, they saw the man in the rowing boat coming back towards them. He called as soon as they were close enough.

"There's no one there! I thought you said you left them on the jetty?"

The Igmopong faces twisted in surprise.

"We did!"

"Well, they're no there."

"They must be."

"Well, they're no. Unless they can stay under water for five minutes."

The distance between the boats was closing rapidly at the corner of the lake.

Doris became suddenly and inexplicably suspicious.

"Who are you, anyway?" she said.

"I'm . . . an uncle," said the stranger.

"Which one's uncle?" demanded Doris.

"Er . . . does it really matter?"

"No," said Cedric. "We—"

"YES," interrupted Doris, with a sideways kick at Cedric's ankle, "it *does* matter. Which one's uncle are you?"

"The one with glasses."

Doris had a flash of inspiration.

"You mean *Billy*?" she said, cunningly.

"That's right," said the man. "Billy. Young Billy."

It was a simple trick, and for once in her life Doris had exhibited some sense. This man was a stranger. She had seen most of the Naitabals' relatives around their houses at one time or another, but she'd never seen this man. There was no telling what he might be up to.

"*Billy*?" said Andy. "Who's Bi—?"

"Shut up!" hissed Doris, digging him in the small of the back with her paddle. Even Cedric had caught on, and he and Doris exchanged knowing glances. Doris mouthed, "Stranger danger!"

Luckily, the man was still far enough away not to have heard the hurried whispers.

"We're coming to see," said Cedric suddenly, as a bright, crafty look flashed across his face. "We know they're at the jetty because that's where we left them."

"Without any arms or legs," said Amanda. "So they can't have gone far."

The stranger turned his boat, and they all rowed to the jetty once again, then tied up the two rafts and the rowing boat. They all climbed out on to the wooden planking. Cedric and the Igmopong were genuinely mystified by the disappearance of the Naitabals. There was a strange gleam in Cedric's eye as he pointed at the thick posts that stood up out of the water all round the house.

"When we saw them last," he said, pointing, "they were walking on the posts round that side. Perhaps there's a way in."

The man was as curious as the Igmopong, and took the hint

from Cedric without the slightest suspicion. He set out, striding from post to post. As soon as he was twenty posts away and out of earshot, Cedric whispered to the others.

"As soon as he's gone round the corner, untie the boats. And be quick. We're taking them all."

Fifteen posts later, still scrutinising the walls of the house and the water round his feet, the man turned the corner and was out of sight of the jetty.

"Now!" whispered Cedric.

Within seconds, Andy and Amanda were on the raft getting ready with the oars, and Doris and Cedric were untying *Naitabal II* and the stranger's rowing boat. In five more seconds they were on their raft, holding the ropes of the captured prizes. Then Andy and Amanda struck the water with their paddles, and the whole flotilla started to move away from the jetty.

"Row straight out!" hissed Cedric. "He might be a good swimmer! Just row straight out!"

Cedric and Doris made the other vessels fast to theirs, then joined in the paddling. The raft picked up speed, and the stranger still hadn't shown.

"We're far enough," said Cedric. "We can start turning now. That way." He pointed, and they swung to starboard, going round Ghost Island in the same direction as the man was walking round on the posts. They had rowed a long way before the stranger reappeared. When he saw where they were, and what they had with them, he exploded into a fit of angry Scottish shouting.

"What d'ya think ya're doin'? Where are ya going with ma boat? Come back here, or I'll be teaching ya somethin'!"

"We told you we were pirates!" Cedric shouted.

The stranger repeated his words over and over again, in different orders, and with a lot of very bad words in between.

Rather than making the Igmopong turn round and go back, the shouting had the opposite effect: the Igmopong paddled even faster. They left the lake and entered the mouth of the river. By the time Ghost Island was out of sight, the man had stopped shouting.

"We've got three boats now," said Cedric, pleased with himself.

"We only need one more," said Doris, "and we'll have a set. One each. I wonder where we can get that one from?"

Andy, who had been thinking, frowned and turned to Doris.

"Why did you say Boff's name was Billy?" he said.

The Naitabals found themselves in a large square hall with doors off to left, right and straight ahead. With the drawbridge closed behind them, there was no natural light. The whole scene was illuminated by a chandelier in the centre of the ceiling and several wall fittings.

Strangely, the first thing they noticed was that it was very clean everywhere – not murky and dusty as they were expecting, considering it had been boarded up for so many years.

They stood in a group, waiting, Toby shivering, wondering what they had let themselves in for. How could they have been so stupid as to come in all together? At least two of them should have stayed outside. But now they were well and truly trapped, a dozen questions tumbled over and over in four of their heads like washing in a tumble drier.

Had they really seen a ghost? How could the drawbridge have opened if no one lived there? Even if anyone did live there, why would they let the Naitabals in? If no one lived there, how was the house so clean and tidy? How did the person get in if there was no boat outside? How did they get their food? How did they get out? Who was it? Did they have permission to be there? Were they crooks trying to hide something? Was there really any treasure here, or had it been taken long, long ago?

The question tumbling over in the fifth head – Toby's – was how quickly he could get out of his soaking clothes and wrap himself up in a curtain. His eyes roamed the room, looking for the curtains that looked the warmest.

While the others were thinking their questions, unable to discuss them in case some stranger might be listening, Toby spotted a thick, velvety candidate and started towards it. His movement – and the others' thoughts – were brought to an abrupt end by a high-pitched voice that startled them back into reality.

"*Get that wet boy in here! Bring him in!*" said the voice. It came from a room to their left.

Slowly, they shuffled towards it and went in, with Toby's feet squelching and trailing wet footmarks.

A woman was standing on a chair at the shuttered window. She had her back to them, and was reaching up and taking down one of the heavy green curtains. She turned with it draped across her arms and stepped down. She was a tall, slim woman of about fifty or fifty-five, with a bright but vague look about her. She smiled and greeted them as if they had been invited for tea.

"There you are, there you are," she said cheerfully. "Sit down, all of you. Do sit down. No, not you," to Toby. "We must get you dried out."

She approached Toby and wrapped the curtain round and round him. Toby, still shivering, thought it was funny that she'd had exactly the same idea as him.

"That'll keep the draught out until we can get your things dried properly," she added. Then she turned to address them all. "I haven't been honoured with so many guests in this house, well . . . ever. In fact, I've never had any guests in this house at all. I usually frighten them away. But falling in the water at this time of year is a serious matter, so you're the first, you see."

The Naitabals introduced themselves, and the woman

asked them where they lived. When she discovered that Boff and Charlotte lived in Brunswick Road, she said, "Isn't that where Mr Marriott, the builder, lives?"

"Do you mean Mr Elliott?" said Boff. "He's our friend. I live next door, and Charlotte lives next-door-but-one on the other side. He built our tree-house for us."

"In that case," said the woman, "you and I are friends, because Mr Melliott is a friend of mine. He did some work for me once. But don't ask me what *my* name is, I've completely forgotten it . . . Oh, no, I haven't. Here it comes . . . It's Smithers, Miss Daphne Smithers. But you can call me Daffy. All my friends call me Daffy, because that's what I am. Not that I've got many friends. None of their names spring to mind just now."

"I'm sure you've lots of friends, Miss Smithers," said Jayne, then added, "Do you . . . do you *live* here?"

"Good gracious, no," said Miss Smithers. "I couldn't possibly live in a place like this. It's haunted, you know."

"Yes, we know," said Charlotte. "We heard that it was haunted. In fact, we think we saw the ghost just now."

"It wouldn't surprise me if you did," said Miss Smithers. "She always appears when people are snooping around the house. She doesn't like visitors, especially if they've come to steal things. You haven't come to steal things, have you?"

"No, Miss Smithers," said Ben. "We'd just like to know more about the house. We'd like to know who owns it, and why it's kept locked up, and that sort of thing, that's all."

"Why don't we all have a nice cup of tea," said Miss Smithers, "and get this young man dried out? I'll tell you all about it. Would you like that?"

"Yes, please, Miss Smithers."

"Come on, then. Follow me."

Miss Smithers waddled quickly from the room, and the Naitabals followed in her wake like ducklings after their mother.

## CHAPTER TWELVE

# *Affy-dang*

"Thank you for letting us in," said Boff. "We were worried when Toby fell in the water."

"I saw what those other children did, of course. You're the first people to be marooned on the jetty. I saw them going off with your boat, so I couldn't leave you out there to starve or freeze to death, could I? The lake water's cold, especially at this time of year, and I thought you might be tempted to swim across. Not a good idea. There's no other house for miles, apart from mine. And then, of course, Tommy fell in."

"Toby, Miss Smithers," said Toby.

"Toby. My memory's terrible these days," said Miss Smithers as she led on.

The Naitabals, still virtually dumb with shock at the sudden change of events, followed Miss Smithers into another panelled room on the east side of the house. They were even more shocked when she pointed an ultrasound control, and a secret panel in front of them opened. It happened in two stages. First, they heard a grinding noise behind the panel, then Miss Smithers pushed the frame of the panelling itself like a door and led them down a flight of steps that led into what looked like a cellar. They calculated that they must be below the level of the water by now. Miss Smithers, talking endlessly, closed the doors behind them, then opened another door in the opposite wall. An incredible sight opened up in front of them.

"*It's a tunnel!*" squealed Charlotte.

"That's right, Catherine," said Miss Smithers, leading them

into it.

"It's Charlotte, Miss Smithers."

"Oh dear, how can I remember Charlotte? I'm the same with everything, people's names, place names, the names of flowers. For instance, what's the flower called that has Father Christmas up against a brick wall?"

"We don't know, Miss," said Charlotte.

"Do call me Daffy – because that's what I am."

"We don't know, Daffy."

"I've nearly got it – Santolina, that's it. Santa *leaning* against a wall."

The Naitabals smiled as Miss Smithers rushed on down the low, narrow tunnel. It was lit with a weak electric bulb every ten metres, so they could easily see where they were going.

"There's another flower that's something to do with dead parrots – *polygonum*, that's it. And another one that reminds me of margarine in a mug."

"Buttercups?" suggested Jayne.

"Clever girl, Joan, thank you!"

"Jayne, Miss Smithers."

"Jayne – how can I remember that? I have such a terrible memory, you know, I bought one of those books that said anyone could have a super power memory. I thought, well, I couldn't possibly have a super power memory, but that's what the advert said, so I thought it must be true. Anyway, I bought the book and it said the best way to remember things was to *visualise*. For instance, when I wanted to remember the name of that flower, Santolina, I thought of Santa leaning against a brick wall. A week later, of course, when I saw the flower again, I had this wonderful picture in my head of the flower growing against a brick wall, with Father Christmas doing press-ups against it. Was it a wallflower? A wallpresser? A Christmas beard? A winter-flowering brick climber?"

"It's a Santolina," said Toby helpfully.

"Yes, I do get them eventually," said Miss Smithers. "But the book was quite wrong, of course. You can only have a super power memory if you've already got a good memory – good enough to remember how to have a super power memory! The author hadn't reckoned with my brain, you see."

Miss Smithers paused for a single breath, then rattled on.

"Most people's brains are like a lovely office with fitted carpets, smart filing cabinets, and bright sunshine coming through the windows. When those brains want to remember something, they find it in a jiffy.

"But my brain's not like that at all. It's an office, yes, but the carpet's dog-eared and coffee-stained, the place is thick with dust, and the filing cabinets have fallen over. All the files have fallen out, and someone's been in and kicked them into a big heap. When I want to remember a name, I have to search through this enormous pile of mixed-up papers, and of course that mixes things up even more."

Miss Smithers was laughing at her own misfortune by now, and the Naitabals felt free to laugh, too, as the tunnel took them down further and further under the lake.

"I went on another course where they promised to improve my memory. The lady was very impressive. As we arrived she was waiting at the door to greet us and she asked for our full names and dates of birth. When we'd all settled down in our seats, about forty of us, she repeated all our names, in alphabetic order, and all our dates of birth, too! Wonderful! Then, of course, she tried to teach us her technique!"

Miss Smithers threw her hands in the air in mock despair, accidentally scraping the roof of the tunnel.

"*She* said the way to do it was to imagine you had a wonderful secretary in your brain – a very efficient secretary. When you want to memorise something, you simply give it to your secretary to file. And when you want it back again, you just ask your secretary for it. Simple.

"Did it work?" said Ben.

"Well, I got a mental secretary all right, a very efficient female. I gave her lots of things to file away, and she seemed to be doing it fine. Then she disappeared. I couldn't find her anywhere. I looked in the office in my brain, and things were just the same as before. Papers strewn everywhere, and no sign of the things I'd asked her to file away. I think she must have gone on holiday and decided not to come back. Hopeless!"

The Naitabals laughed again. The tunnel had started climbing now, and they were all getting breathless trying to keep up with their hostess.

"So when I try to name things, you'll have to help me find the right words," said Miss Smithers, as they finally reached the bottom of several steep flights of stone steps. They led up to a strong wooden door that was standing ajar.

At the top, Miss Smithers turned off the tunnel lights and shepherded the Naitabals through the door, where they found themselves in the cellar of another house. She locked the door and led them up wooden steps into a sitting-room.

"Here we are!" she cooed cheerfully. "Let's get Tommy – no! – Toby! – I'll have to think of you with one of those jugs on your head – dried out. Then I'll make some tea. Bread and jam and hot drinks, I think!"

"Thank you, Miss Smithers."

"Daffy, please!"

When Toby's clothes were drying on the radiators, with Toby wrapped in two warm dressing gowns, they settled down for tea.

"Who owns the house on the lake, Daffy?" said Charlotte.

"Ghost Island? That's a bit of a mystery in itself. It used to be owned by a man called – think of a piece of cheese – a wedge – Reg!"

The Naitabals exchanged interested glances, remembering that the letter that accompanied Peter's original code had been signed by someone called Reg.

"His second name was something to do with the captain of a ship . . . I can see the captain standing there – in fact, two captains . . ."

"Sailor? Tailor?" said Jayne.

"Commander?" said Toby.

"Admirals?" said Charlotte.

"Masters?" said Boff.

"That's it! Masters. Reg Masters. I don't know whether Reg Masters was a good man or a bad man, but he always treated me like a lady. Nevertheless, he was arrested one night and the police locked him up, and the next morning he was dead in his cell. Heart attack, they said – I think. It might have been a stroke, but I think they said it was his heart."

"So what happened to the house?" said Jayne.

"Well, that was fourteen years ago. He left a will, but there's been such a mighty mix-up – a bit like my brain – that's there's been a to-do ever since, and they can't settle it. So the house is boarded up for safety, and I still keep it clean and keep the snoopers away. Mr . . . Masters still pays me every month regular as clockwork, so I keep looking after it. And so I shall until somebody tells me not to."

"How can he pay you if he's . . . dead?" said Toby.

"The money comes in regularly, that's all that bothers me."

Charlotte suddenly plucked up the courage to ask the audacious question she'd been storing up.

"We'd *love* to have a proper look at the house on Ghost Island," she said, glancing at the others, and feeling her cheeks going red. It was bold, but it could be their only chance ever to see what the secret coded letter was trying to tell them.

Miss Smithers' answer was more than they could have

dreamed of.

"Why don't you stay there the night?" she said, and Charlotte felt so pleased she gasped with surprise. "There isn't much room in my little house here, but there's plenty of room over there. I think you'd be thrilled to spend the night on Ghost Island, am I right?"

"Yes!"

"Yes, Daffy!"

"Yes!"

"What about the ghosts?" said Jayne, still worried.

Miss Smithers laughed and offered them more sandwiches.

"We saw the ghost," said Charlotte. "And we heard the crying . . ."

Miss Smithers laughed again and topped up their drinks.

"The house really is haunted, you know," she said. "But I have to help it along a bit."

"But why?"

"It's my job. I have to keep people away from the house. Someone tried to burgle it one night, but I was ready for them. They were so frightened they crashed their car."

"We heard about that," said Toby. "How did you do it?"

"Ah, that's a secret!" said Miss Smithers.

"We wouldn't tell," said Ben. "We promise. Naitabals never tell secrets."

But Miss Smithers wouldn't say any more.

"Daffy," said Boff suddenly, "do you know what Reg Masters was arrested for?"

"Oh, yes. There was a robbery. A big robbery. An armoured van delivering new sovereigns from the Royal Mint was hijacked. Tens of thousands of gold sovereigns were taken. There were only two men involved. The police had no idea who the other one was, and I don't know why they thought the owner of Ghost Island had anything to do with it. But they arrested him, and he died."

"If he did do it, Miss Smithers, do you think he would have

hidden the sovereigns on Ghost Island?"

Miss Smithers laughed again.

"I don't think so, my dears," she said. "The police searched the place from top to bottom. If *they* couldn't find anything, who could?"

The Naitabals looked at each other and grinned.

"Mind you, they didn't find the tunnel . . ." Miss Smithers continued. "The panelling is backed with stone so it doesn't sound hollow, and it can only be opened with my gadget."

"Ultrasound," put in Boff.

"Ultrasound, that's right. What was the name of the man in charge? He came up here and asked a lot of questions, asking if I'd seen anything, but he never knew about the tunnel. What was his name? My brain's giving me a picture of Cinderella trying on one of her glass slippers.

"Mr Slipper?" suggested Jayne.

"Mr Glass?" suggested Charlotte.

"Mr Cinders?" suggested Ben.

"Mr Pumpkin?" said Toby.

"It'll come to me," said Daffy. "I'll think of it eventually."

"May I ask you something else?" said Boff.

"Of course."

"How do you know when people are on the island, or on the lake? You can't even see the lake from here, can you? I looked out of the windows. The house is in a hollow, and surrounded by trees as well."

"That's easy," said Miss Smithers. "Ghost Island has a system that watches the lake for hot things that move – like human bodies. Infra blue, or something."

"Infra red?" suggested Boff.

"Yes, something like that. If anyone's on the lake near the house, a buzzer goes off and a red light flashes. Well, when the owner, Mr . . . Masters – asked me to keep the house clean and look after it, he extended the wires to my house as well. So if anyone goes on the lake, the buzzer buzzes in my bedroom, and a red light flashes. It only takes me a few minutes to go down the tunnel to see if anyone needs frightening off."

"How can you see, when it's all boarded up?" said Jayne.

"I'm sure you'll find that out for yourselves!" said Miss Smithers. "Now. We need to telephone your parents, I think. And staying the night will give you a bit more time to get your raft back as well, won't it?"

"Thank you, Miss Smithers!"

The Naitabals were almost too thrilled to speak. Suddenly, the adventure was taking on a new and exciting dimension. Not only would they be able to explore Ghost Island properly, they'd actually have all night to search it from top to bottom. It would be a real challenge to see if they could find anything that the police might have missed all those years ago.

"We'll call your parents now," said Miss Smithers, fetching the telephone. "I'll speak to them if you want me to. I'll tell them Freddie Merriott's a good friend of mine, and he knows me. You can tell them that no one can get into Ghost Island, because you can lock yourself in, and that's true. Don't mention the tunnel, though, because that's a secret, but it *can* be locked at both ends."

Miss Smithers smiled and looked at each of their faces in turn.

"You can't possibly come to any harm over there," she added.

## CHAPTER THIRTEEN

# *The Message*

The bearded man stood on the posts where he could see the entrance of the river, watching and waiting. He waited for five minutes, ten minutes, half expecting the pirates to return with his boat and share a laugh at his expense. He soon realised that they weren't coming back. He was now in the same position that the children had found themselves in earlier. They had disappeared without much delay, so the decision they had made was probably the same as his. Except that he had one advantage. *He* knew exactly how far it was to the nearest house, and exactly where it was. Had the five children who'd disappeared known it as well?

His mind flew back nearly fourteen years. He remembered the house, tucked up in the woods that surrounded the lake, hidden from it by the trees and the hollow it stood in. He remembered paying it a visit all those years ago, asking the occupant – a woman of forty-ish – if she had noticed any activity on the lake that night? Had she taken a stroll? Had she seen any comings, or goings, on Ghost Island? Did she know the man who owned the house?

The house was only two hundred plus metres from the shore – if you knew which way to swim and where to find it – and that's where the children must have gone. They must have been good swimmers.

He took off all his clothes except his underpants, placed his watch in the middle, and rolled everything into a bundle. He took a deep breath and lowered himself into the deep, dark water, keeping his head well above the surface. His teeth started chattering from the shocking cold. He lifted the roll of clothes from the jetty, held them aloft with one hand, then began a steady three-limbed breast-stroke towards the shore.

It seemed an age. As he swam, the water gripped his body tighter and tighter in its freezing vice, but at last his feet were kicking the sandy bottom and he was standing up and wading ashore. Shivering violently, he dried himself off with his vest, then donned his dry clothes as quickly as he could. Once dressed, he strode into the margin of the wood, heading briskly along a deer track that led roughly in the right direction. He already felt warm again by the time he reached the house, where he rang the bell and knocked on the door for several minutes. There was no answer, even though he could see a light glowing somewhere inside. In the woods all around him, the light was already fading to dusk. He wasted no more time, but turned on his heel and strode in the rough direction of another house: the more distant house where he had parked his car and borrowed his boat – the boat that had now been stolen by the stupid pirate children.

He would be back tomorrow.

As soon as the wall panel swung closed and they heard the bolts snap into place, the Naitabals felt a peculiar excitement scurrying through their veins. They explored the house immediately, moving in a group from room to room, calling out their discoveries in triumphant voices.

"Look!" said Ben. "There are slots in the shutters! We can see out, but no one can see in!"

It was true. Although the windows had been boarded up on the outside, slots the size of letterboxes had been left at every window. It was possible to look out at any part of the lake, or the jetty, or at any of the posts that surrounded the house and protected it from inquisitive boaters.

"We can see if anyone approaches," said Ben, "and they can't see us."

"They'd be able to see if we put lights on at night," said Charlotte. "Rule number one: if we put lights on in any rooms tonight, we must draw the curtains first."

"Why don't we just draw all the curtains anyway," said Toby. "Then we can put lights on and off as we need them."

"That's a good idea," said Jayne. "And then if we want to spy out, we just turn off the light in that room first."

The plan was agreed and they immediately set about drawing all the curtains and then switching on most of the lights in the whole house so they could explore with ease.

"What are we looking for?" said Ben.

"We don't know," said Boff. He took the message from his pocket and read it out loud. *"The southern secret is the hiding place grid ref 261626 Treasure Island."*

"Well, we're at map reference 261 east 626 north already," said Charlotte, "so we're looking for the Southern Secret, whatever that is."

"It's funny it says 'Treasure Island' instead of 'Ghost Island'," said Jayne. "I mean, it's definitely called Ghost Island because it says so on the map."

"I think it's just a teaser," said Ben. "I think Treasure Island sounds much more exciting. It's telling us there's treasure here, that's what it's doing."

"I'm not so sure," said Boff. "We'll have to wait and see."

They explored methodically, starting in the sitting-room. The house was still fully furnished and carpeted. There were pictures on the walls, ornaments on shelves and in niches, and books in the bookcases.

When they had finished a thorough search of the sitting-room they were already beginning to wonder if there was anything left to be found.

"I bet someone found it years ago," said Toby, "and took it away."

"I can't really see that we can find anything the police didn't find," said Jayne. "They search very thoroughly when they search a criminal's house. They even take up floorboards and knock down walls if they think there's something there."

"We've got to be cleverer than the police, then," said Boff. "They only thought there *might* be something here when *they* searched. But we *know* there's something here."

"The police didn't even find the entrance to the tunnel," said Ben. "Miss Smithers said so. So they can't have been that clever, can they?"

"That entrance is really brilliant, though," said Charlotte. "No one could ever guess there was anything there."

"No," said Jayne. "Even if you tap the panel it doesn't sound hollow behind."

"Perhaps there's somewhere else like that," said Ben. "Somewhere even Daffy doesn't know about. Perhaps it opens a cupboard instead of a tunnel."

"Even if we found one," said Boff, "we'd need the right ultrasound code to open it. But it's still worth looking."

The entrance was so good, it was impossible to say whether there was another place on the panelling where a hiding place might be. As they moved from room to room, they found no more panelling, and no trace of trap-doors, hidden cupboards, or safes behind pictures.

At the end of three hours they had searched every possible hiding place, short of taking up carpets and knocking down walls, and found nothing more exciting than a massive spider. It was getting late by this time, and they were hungry. Miss Smithers had provided them with cereal for supper, and they finished it off with a hot drink before choosing which rooms they would sleep in.

Jayne and Charlotte chose a room on the first floor, and Boff, Ben and Toby decided to remain close by in the one next door. They talked long into the evening in the haunted house to keep their spirits up. It was only when Ben announced that it was two o'clock in the morning that they realised they would have to have some sleep if they were going to get up first thing and start searching the house again.

Toby, who usually slept in half the morning, was still wide awake when the others had gone to bed and their breathing had settled to a quiet rhythm. They had left all the lights on in the house to comfort them against visits from ghosts, and when Toby saw that it was 3am he raised himself from his bed and walked quietly round all the rooms in the house. He finished up at the big bookcase in the sitting-room, picked out a book that looked interesting and took it up to his room. He lay down, reading it sideways, balancing it on the pillow. By the time he had read the first two pages, his eyes drooped, the book slipped from his hands and he, too, was fast asleep.

Morning came with a shout from Charlotte.

"Hey! It's eight-fifteen! Get up, everybody – we've got to search the house again. We haven't got much time now!"

One by one they stirred, except Toby, who was buried under an avalanche of pillows and sheets and blankets, and didn't look as if he'd be eating breakfast with them.

The other four set to work in the kitchen preparing food, and by nine o'clock the house was back the way they had found it – beds made, crockery washed up and stored, and everything neat and tidy – except Toby.

"I'll put his book back," said Charlotte, leaning over his motionless body and taking it. "Aren't I kind?"

They didn't disturb him, but began their second search one Naitabal short.

"Where could they hide gold sovereigns where even the police wouldn't find them?" said Boff. "It doesn't make sense." He took the code translation from his pocket again and read it aloud to the others. "'*The southern secret is the hiding place grid ref 261 626 Treasure Island.*' This is map reference 261 east 626 north, so this must be Treasure Island. The sovereigns have got to be here – but where?"

"What about on the roof?" said Jayne.

"If it was on the roof the police would have found it," said Ben. "I bet."

"What about the attic, then?"

"There isn't one," said Charlotte. "The upstairs ceilings all go straight up to the rafters."

"In the lake, then," said Jayne. "Under the water."

"Mmmm, it's possible," said Boff. "But let's face it, *we'll* never find it if it's under the water. And if it was thousands of gold sovereigns you can be sure the police would have sent frogmen round the whole lake with metal detectors. No – there's got to be somewhere else . . ."

Boff's words suddenly trailed off as he noticed the others staring over his shoulder. He turned his head to follow their gaze, and saw a strange apparition standing in the doorway.

It was Toby. He had woken up at last. He was standing like a waxwork dummy that had sleep-walked its way to the room. He looked as if he wanted to say something, but hadn't yet engaged the speaking part of his brain.

"Toby!" said Charlotte, shocked. "What's the matter? You look as if you've seen another ghost!"

"It's the book—" he said, and stopped.

"The one you were reading last night? Yes – I put it back. Do you want me to fetch it?"

"No." Toby's mind seemed to be stirring at last. He moved two paces towards them. "I thought I heard someone say something about Treasure Island?"

"I did," said Boff. "I was just reading out the coded message again, that's all."

Toby blinked twice.

"It's the book," he said again, and stopped again.

"I told you—" Charlotte began, but Ben interrupted her.

"Do you mean Treasure Island is the *book*?" he said, still

staring at Toby.

"The book I put back wasn't *Treasure Island*," Charlotte began again, "it was—" but Toby interrupted her this time.

"No," he said. "I mean I saw it – last night. *Treasure Island.* I was looking for something to read and didn't really notice anything. But this morning when I heard Boff say it, I remembered, like a dream. I saw it in the bookcase." He pointed. "That one over there. *Treasure Island.*"

Four heads turned to where Toby was pointing, and five pairs of legs moved towards the tall glass-fronted bookcase that took up most of the wall at one side of the sitting-room. Jayne reached it first, and she stretched up to open the door as her bright blue eyes scanned the shelves.

"There!" said Toby, pushing past them.

They all followed his movement as he reached over to the left side of a shelf near the middle. They all saw the gold lettering on its spine and read the title even before Toby's hand circled round it: *R.L.Stevenson – Treasure Island.*

In the same breathless moment, they all realised what it could mean.

"That's why the message doesn't say map reference whatever-it-is *Ghost Island*!" Charlotte squealed. "It must say map reference whatever-it-is *Treasure Island* because, because – *quick, Toby! – let's see if there's a message inside!*"

Eagerly, but carefully, Toby opened the little book that was over seventy years old. On the first blank page a name was written neatly in pen: Reg Masters.

"Look at the handwriting!" squealed Jayne. "It's the same as the writing in the letter that came with the secret message from Peter!"

But as Toby turned the pages it quickly became clear that there was nothing else in the book. They had all expected a piece of paper to fall out with another message on it. Instead, their faces fell in bitter disappointment. They'd found *Treasure Island*, but it was empty.

Toby turned every single page to make sure, but nothing was inside the book apart from the name of the owner – the owner of Ghost Island – the man who had died in police custody all those years ago – the man who had written the original secret message and the letter – Reg Masters.

Suddenly Charlotte had an idea. She took the book from Toby and carefully opened it wide, gently easing back the boards until the spine cover buckled outwards. She could just see down the narrow shaft between the spine cover and the binding. She held it up to the light.

"Oh," she said, disappointed again. "Nothing there. I thought there might be something hidden behind the spine."

Ben took the book from her hands and had a turn at looking through it again. Then Jayne did the same, then Boff. None of them could see anything written anywhere.

At last Toby's turn came back again. The excitement had woken him up properly, and like the others he turned pages backwards and forwards, convinced they must have missed something.

"Perhaps two pages have got stuck together," he said. "Perhaps it was done on purpose so even the police wouldn't find anything."

He started turning the pages again from the beginning, checking that the page numbers followed in sequence, with none missing. The pages of the preface were in Roman numerals, and they all helped to check them. The story itself started on page three, and Toby began counting the odd pages aloud.

"Three, five, seven . . ."

When he reached thirty-seven he suddenly stopped and turned back a page. The others were galvanised.

"What?"

"Toby, tell us!"

"What have you found?"

Toby flicked more pages, then went back to the beginning of the book again.

"Toby – what is it?" An urgent request from Charlotte.

"Just a minute," he said. "I think—"

Much to everyone's frustration he stopped, but then suddenly started again.

"Yes – Boff – look! Jayne! Ben! Charlotte! Look!"

He opened the book at page three and pushed a dirty fingernail towards the top of the page. They all peered over.

"What?"

"Look!" Toby said again. "Look at this word."

At last they could see what Toby was talking about. The first word on the sixth line had a faint pencil mark underlining it.

"See?" he said. "The first word on that line – *lifted* – is underlined." Toby turned the next page. "Page five – look, a third of the way down the page. The first word – *only* – it's underlined."

"Toby, you're absolutely brilliant!" shouted Boff, who rarely raised his voice. "Come on," he said, turning to the others, "who's got pencil and paper?"

"We all have," said Ben. "We're all wearing Naitabal battledress – remember?"

It was unusual for Boff's sharp brain to be addled, but there was so much excitement in the air, it had got through to him as well. Moments later he had his emergency writing materials at the ready, and was jotting down the words as Toby called them out.

*"Lifted, only, which, it, bless, was, Jim, a, addressed, wrist, croaking, overcoming . . ."*

"Stop there a minute," said Boff. His hand moved quickly over the piece of paper, trying things out. It wasn't the words themselves – they didn't make sense. Was it the first letter of each word? He turned to Toby again.

"Did you say it's always the *first* word that's underlined?"

"Yep."

"But the first word on different lines each time?"

"Yep."

"Don't bother to tell me the words, then," said Boff. "It's nothing to do with the words themselves – it can't be. It would be too much of a coincidence if all the words he needed happened to be the first word on every line. No. Tell me which *line* they're on . . . Count the lines."

Toby turned back to the third page and started again, carefully counting the lines until he reached the underlined word.

"It's six lines down on page three," he said. "Twelve down on page five. Then three. Then ten. Ten again. Twenty-four, seven, fifteen, twelve, two, three . . ."

"That's enough to test it," said Boff.

The others looked on, fascinated, as Boff wrote down the numbers, then wrote underneath them the corresponding letters of the alphabet:

```
6 12 3 10 10 24 7 15 12 2 3
F  L C  J  J  X G  O  L B C
```

Then he wrote the letters again, shifting them one to the right. He added them up, then, using the same method he'd used for the original coded message.

"It works!" he shouted. "Look!" He turned his paper so the others could see the result:

```
    F L C J J X G O L B C
+     F L C J J X G O L B C
  -------------------------
=   F R O M T H E V A N E
```

They were all so excited now that everyone tried to grab the book off Toby to look up the next set of line numbers. But Toby held firm, and another ten minute's careful work produced the full code from the copy of *Treasure Island*:

```
FLCJJ XGOLB CCLII YVRLF YEVRL BGGXO
PDNQB CXVYG HJJOE RWVSB RP
```

They all set to work offsetting letters and adding them up the way Boff had shown them, and it was amidst great excitement that Boff read out the final solution.

"*From the vane four hundred and nine metres east forty two south*," he said. "That's what it says."

"That was all very complicated," said Jayne, when the excitement had started to die down. "Why didn't he just underline the letters he wanted?"

"That's easy," said Boff. "The police, or anyone else, could have found the book. This way, they wouldn't be able to read the message unless they knew the secret code."

"I know where the weather vane is," said Ben. "It's on one of the chimneys. It's shaped like a cockerel with the compass points on it. It looked like a good place to throw a grappling hook if you wanted to climb the walls."

"That's where we go from, then," said Charlotte. "Four hundred and nine metres east of there, and forty-two south."

"How are we going to measure four hundred and nine metres east?" said Jayne. "There's water all round the house, we haven't got a tape measure, we haven't got a boat, and we can't walk on water. It's impossible."

They all turned to Boff.

He looked at their expectant faces one by one and then gave a little grin.

"It's easy," he said. "Come on – I'll show you."

## CHAPTER FOURTEEN

# *The Southern Secret*

Before the Naitabals finally left Ghost Island, they were determined to put everything back the way they had found it. First, they replaced the copy of *Treasure Island.* They certainly didn't want to leave it out for someone else to find – even though no one else would have much chance of solving the secret message inside. After that, they cleaned and tidied everything else.

At last they were ready, assembled in Naitabal battledress at the entrance to the tunnel. Jayne opened the door and they all trooped through the open panel in the wall. Toby came last and firmly closed the secret entrance.

Once inside Daffy's house, she made them sit down and have what she called a 'proper breakfast'. Then Ben asked the vital question that all the other Naitabals knew needed asking.

"Daffy – ?"

"Yes, Bill?"

"I'm Ben."

"Oh, yes, I was thinking of two flowerpot men. I knew you were one or the other. Yes, Ben?"

"Is it all right if we explore the woods between here and Ghost Island? I mean – do they belong to you, or did they belong to Mr Masters?"

"Oh, help yourself. The whole lake and two hundred acres of the woods belong to Ghost Island. I'm looking after it, so I can easily give you permission. There, I've given it!"

"Thank you, Miss Smithers."

"Thank you, Daffy."

"Thanks!"

Daffy insisted on them leaving the washing up, and made them telephone all their parents to tell them they were safe and would be spending another day with their new friend. She made them packed lunches, then finally set them free into the woods.

"There are just a couple of other things . . ." said Boff before they parted.

"Yes, B . . ."

"Boff."

"Yes, Boff?"

"May we please borrow a metal tape measure, if you have one – and a big ball of string?"

"Of course. I've got both."

While the Naitabals waited on the path, she disappeared inside the house again, re-emerging moments later with the things Boff had asked for. Then she pointed the way for them and waved them goodbye.

The Naitabals walked round the side of the house, down some steep brick steps, fighting off brambles that clutched at them through the overgrown hedge as they passed. They turned left on to an indistinct path, climbed to the rim of the bowl that encircled the house, then dropped downhill through the woods until they reached the shore of the lake.

The water was flat calm, with no sign of human life, and only a few ducks and moorhens to make ripples in the distance. The house on Ghost Island stared at them with its blindfolded windows as if it was sitting there, waiting for a game of blind man's buff.

"Okay, Boff," said Charlotte. "How did you say we were going to measure this distance of four hundred and nine metres from the weather vane?"

The four of them stood looking at Boff as if he was a conjuror about to perform a magic trick. With just a metal rule in his pocket, a ball of string – and no boat – he was going to measure this distance of four hundred and nine metres due east of the weather vane on the house that stood in the middle of the lake. It *was* a magic trick.

"I know," said Ben. "He's going to measure the right length of string, swim out to the island with it, climb up and fix it to the vane, then swim back with the string in his teeth."

The others laughed.

"We don't even have to go near Ghost Island," said Boff. "First, though, we'll have to walk *that* way." He pointed, herding them like sheep along the shore for a while. Then he stopped.

The others watched, fascinated, as Boff walked back and forth along the water's edge. He turned this way and that, then peered at Ghost Island, then walked a bit more, then stopped again. Finally, he took out his binoculars, and pointed them in the direction of the weather vane.

"Here's about right," he said. "How far do you think we are from Ghost Island?"

"You're supposed to be measuring, not guessing," protested Jayne.

"Guess first," said Boff. "Measure after."

They all had a guess and Boff added them up and divided the result by five.

"That's an average guess of two hundred and forty metres," said Boff, then immediately started issuing commands. "Jayne – stand here where I am and don't move. Ben – measure me a length of string a hundred and sixty-nine metres long."

As they set to work, Boff began walking backwards, making sure he kept Jayne in a straight line between himself and Ghost Island until he collided with a tree.

"What are you doing, Boff?" said Toby, who couldn't stand the suspense any more. "It all looks like mumbo-jumbo to me."

"I've measured the string," called Ben, standing with massive coils of it draped over his arm.

Boff called from up the slope.

"Okay. Give one end to Jayne and bring the other end to me."

Ben did as he was asked, but when he reached Boff there was still plenty of slack. Leaving Jayne behind, the four of them continued up the hill until the string was as taut as they could get it.

"Toby, can you run down and tell Jayne to come up now?" said Boff. "You can roll up the string as you come."

"What does it all mean?" said Charlotte at last, when Jayne and Toby were back with them.

"All it means," said Boff, "is that we are *roughly* four hundred and nine metres from Ghost Island, due east."

"I think I see," said Charlotte. "You took our guesses of two hundred and forty and added a hundred and sixty-nine to make four hundred and nine. But what about the due east? How do you know that?"

Boff handed her the binoculars.

"Look at the weather vane," he said. "It's pointing straight at us."

Charlotte looked through the eyepieces and moved from side to side the way Boff had done down on the shore.

"So it is!" she squealed. "Clever!"

"But what about the *accurate* four hundred and nine metres?" said Jayne. "How do we do that?"

"That's where the fun begins," said Boff. "Find me some long, straight, strong sticks that we can bang in the ground. I need six."

The sticks were found, and Boff used a fat log to bang the first one in the ground where they were standing. He called it Stick A, tied a string to it, then measured twelve metres on the string, and sent Jayne with it back towards Ghost Island. Keeping Jayne and Stick A in line with the island, he then told Jayne to bang in Stick B.

"Now we want Stick C due south of Stick A," said Boff, "so we need a right angle at Stick A." Boff tied another string to Stick A, measured nine metres on it, and sent Toby roughly south. "Now, Ben, measure a string fifteen metres from Stick B," Boff continued, "and move Toby until both strings meet, then bang in Stick C. That'll be due south."

"Pythagoras," murmured Charlotte. "$9^2 + 12^2 = 15^2$. At least I know that much."

"Now trust me," said Boff. "Continue the line south another thirty-three metres and bang in Stick D."

"Done it!" came the call from Jayne.

"Now come back north from Stick D four point two metres and bang in Stick E."

"Okay!"

Boff and Charlotte were standing at Stick D now. He sent Charlotte off with forty metres of string in the direction of Ghost Island. When the island, Charlotte and Boff were in a straight line, and they'd checked with right angles that Charlotte was exactly west of Stick E, Boff gave the final command to Charlotte, "Bang in Stick F!"

"Is that it?" said Jayne. "Do we know how far we are from Ghost Island now?" She said it half-jokingly, but Boff's face was serious.

"Yes, we do," he said. "All we have to do is measure the distance between Stick E and Stick F and multiply it by ten."

"Boff!"

"Go on, do it," Boff couldn't help smiling. "You'll see!"

Jayne stretched a piece of string between the two sticks. With Toby and Ben's help, she then went along, carefully measuring the length. "It's thirty eight point eight metres," she announced at last.

"Excellent!" said Boff. "That means Stick A is exactly three hundred and eighty-eight metres from the vane. If we go twenty-one metres east from Stick D, we'll be at our target! 'X' marks the spot!"

"Boff," said Jayne, "I know this is maths, not magic – but how does it work?"

"It's trigonometry," said Boff. "Really useful stuff." He drew a diagram of what they had done.

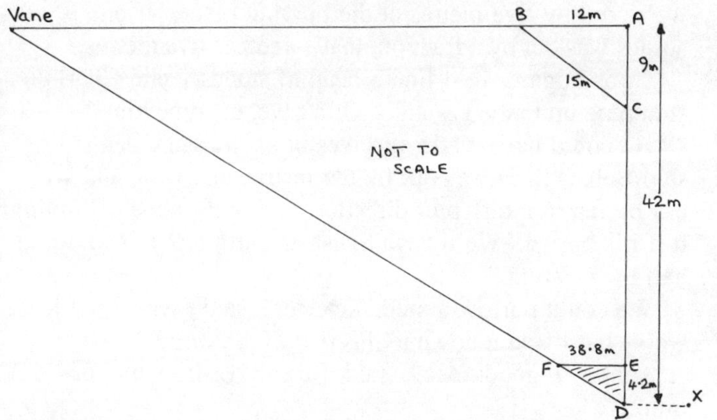


"All it means is that the little shaded triangle FED is the same *shape*, but *one tenth the size* of the big triangle from Ghost Island to Stick A to Stick D. So if we know how far it is from E to F, we know that Stick A is ten times as far from the vane, don't we?"

Boff felt really pleased with their efforts, and all the others suddenly realised that they quite liked trigonometry, too.

When they had finished the final measurement of twenty-one metres to the east of stick 'D' they found themselves in a part of the wood that looked much like any other. The trees were well spread out, and there was plenty of grass and undergrowth in between. The spot where Ben was standing with the string in one hand and the last stick in the other was very close to a large clump of brambles. But there was no other feature, and no obvious reason for choosing such a place to bury a haul of gold sovereigns.

"What do we do now?" said Ben. "Dig?"

Boff was frowning, and all the others were shrugging and wondering what to do.

"It's too inaccurate," said Boff, "that's the trouble. We only have to be out by half a metre with one of our measurements, and by the time we've multiplied by ten, we're out by five metres at the burying place. If one of our angles was out by a fraction, that's another five metres."

"I was hoping we'd find a heap of stones," said Charlotte, slumping on to the ground. "Or a cave, or something."

"He could have made mistakes in *his* measurements, too," said Ben. "If *he* was out by ten metres one way, and we're out by ten in a different direction, we've no hope of finding it if it's buried. We'd have to use an earth mover and dig up half the clearing."

"We could borrow a metal detector," said Jayne. "At least we've narrowed it down to this part of the wood."

"That's a good idea," said Ben. "Boff, what do you think?"

Boff was still frowning and unhappy.

"I didn't think he'd be so *imprecise*," he said after a few seconds thought. "When he says forty-two metres south, it's precise to the nearest metre. But his secret code – that's so precise, you can't mistake it once you know how. If the message was supposed to lead his accomplice – the Bad Man – to the loot, he can't just lead him to the middle of a bramble bush. It's got to be *precise*, hasn't it? He wouldn't be vague about the final hiding place, would he?"

"The *southern secret* is the hiding place," said Jayne suddenly. "I never understood that bit."

"None of us understand that bit," said Charlotte. I can't think how it can help, either. We've travelled south the forty-two metres and here we are in a bramble bush."

"I don't suppose . . ." began Jayne, but Charlotte had carried on speaking at the same time.

"Before we kill ourselves excavating brambles," Charlotte

continued, "why don't we recheck our measurements? Extend the first two sticks—"

"A and B," put in Ben.

" – extend them the full four hundred and nine metres, then check our angles before coming south forty-two metres."

They had a break for refreshments, then spent what was left of the morning rechecking measurements and angles and approaching it the way Charlotte had suggested. As a result, their final stick moved a few metres. It took them to the middle of the bramble patch.

"Oh dear," said Charlotte. "Surely not?"

They stood in an untidy group, gazing at the middle of the tangled briar, wondering how on earth they were going to dig a hole there. Boff started shaking his head and repeating what he had said earlier.

"It's too inaccurate," he said firmly. "Reg Masters could have been out by ten metres – and we could as well. There has to be something more *definite*, not just chancy measurements a quarter of a mile from the house."

I think burying it would be dodgy anyway," said Toby. "The police would just sweep in a big line with metal detectors and find it straight away."

"That's a point," said Ben. "Burying it isn't such a good idea, after all."

Jayne was still thinking.

"What about the *southern secret*?" she said. "You know how we found *Treasure Island* really meant the book, not Ghost Island. Well – no one's explained about the *southern secret*, yet."

"Jayne's right," said Ben. "The southern secret doesn't mean anything on its own. Why not just say 'The hiding place is in Treasure Island'. It doesn't say that, it says *the southern secret* is the hiding place."

"Perhaps it's south from here," said Charlotte and Toby simultaneously, then Toby added, "Let's carry on in a straight line and see what's there."

It was easy enough. All they had to do was go back and look along the new line of sticks. They discovered that the first object that stood in the way in a southerly direction was a small silver birch tree.

"It's too young," said Charlotte. "I bet it wasn't even *born* fourteen years ago."

"Perhaps he planted it over the treasure," said Toby.

"So we've got to uproot a *tree* to get it?" said Charlotte. "Pretty likely."

"He didn't want to make it *too* easy," said Toby.

Ben was looking round in all directions.

"What else is there?" he said. "There's no pile of stones . . ."

"That would be too obvious," said Toby.

" . . .There's a few big oak trees, a few silver birches, an old horse chestnut, and those others I don't know the names of. There's nothing else to mark the spot."

"And if a tree marks the spot," Charlotte repeated, "We've got no chance of digging it up."

"The *southern secret* is the hiding place . . ." Jayne murmured again. "If it was a *crossword*, we'd be trying to get an anagram out of it . . ."

Four pairs of eyes turned to Jayne, and they all became electrified, as if Jayne had switched on their Christmas lights. They all hauled paper and pencils from the pockets of their Naitabal battledress, wrote down the letters of 'southern secret', and started jumbling them up to make new words.

"I get *Cure street nosh*," said Toby.

"*Reset scent hour*," said Jayne.

"*She curse rotten*," said Ben.

"*Score nuts there*," said Toby.

"Here's one for Toby," said Charlotte. "*Test snore cure*!"

They all shouted suggestions as they found them, except Boff, who would only say anything if he thought it was the answer they needed.

"*True hen corsets*," said Toby, laughing. "For fat hens."

"*The curser stone*," said Jayne.

"*Then scour trees*," said Charlotte. "Getting warmer!"

"*No Tresure Chest!*" said Ben. "I know it's not spelt right, but it might mean we're wasting our time . . ."

"You're right," said Charlotte. "I've got, *Curses, not there!*"

They discovered that there were an amazing number of anagrams from the two words, but none that really helped. Then Boff suggested including the word 'the' as well.

"Try all three words," he said. "*The southern secret*."

"*See three cuts north*," said Charlotte almost immediately. It was a good enough suggestion to send them all northwards, looking for three cuts, or ancient scars, on a tree, where someone might have marked it. But they found no cuts, and went back to their pencils and paper.

"*Rush cheese tent rot*," said Toby, laughing.

"*Three cheers to nuts*," said Ben.

"*Rent the cute horses*," said Jayne.

"*See hot chest return*," said Charlotte.

"*Hunt chest rose tree*," said Jayne.

Then Charlotte suddenly screamed.

"I've got it!" she said. She sprang to her feet and started leaping around. She flung her pencil and paper to the ground, performed an enormous pirouette, then clenched her fists and pointed to the biggest tree in sight.

"Charlotte, what is it?" shouted Jayne.

Charlotte turned to them with the biggest grin they'd ever seen in their lives on anyone.

"*Horse chestnut tree!*" she screamed. "It's *horse chestnut tree!*"

All heads immediately swivelled to the huge conker tree that stood at one edge of the clearing. Its main trunk was missing from halfway up, long since struck by lightning or toppled by a great storm. New branches had sprung out from its crown perhaps fifty years before, so now it stood in the shape of an enormous letter 'Y'.

"Charlotte, you're a genius!"

"No, Jayne's the genius. She thought of doing anagrams!"

They ran to the tree, full of happiness and excitement.

Further up in the wood, looking through binoculars, the bearded stranger allowed himself a smile.

## CHAPTER FIFTEEN

# *Scuppered*

The Igmopong's morning had not been a happy one. First, Amanda and Andy had been dragged off on a shopping expedition for new footwear, and by the time they returned it was already past eleven.

During the agonising delay, Cedric and Doris's consciences (normally hibernating) had been pricking them. There had been no sign of any of the Naitabals since the Igmopong had left them stranded on Ghost Island.

"If they've died of cold," said Doris, "it'll be *your* fault! You'll be a *murderer*!"

The other thing that was irritating Cedric – apart from Doris – was the discovery that one of the drums on the first raft they had stolen had started to leak. It hadn't mattered much at first, but now it was beginning to list to one side. The sooner he could do a deal with the Naitabals over a stay in their tree-house, the quicker he could give it back to them. He'd decided to keep *Naitabal II*.

The only problem was, how could he do a deal with the Naitabals when he didn't know where they were? It was very odd how they had disappeared without trace. He had called on Boff's parents, Charlotte's parents, Toby's parents and Ben's parents, but none of them would give him any information. Jayne's parents had refused even to open their front door to him. The truth was, the Naitabals had all given their parents strict instructions never to tell the Igmopong anything. So Cedric had come up against a stone wall.

Soon after eleven, when Andy and Amanda arrived, Mrs Morgan provided them with packed lunches and big wet kisses, and Mr Morgan meekly obeyed orders and drove them to the place where they had hidden the boats.

"I see you've got three boats now," said Mr Morgan, as he dropped them off. "You make them ever so quickly, don't you? Are you making another one today, so you've got one each? Is that it?"

"No," said Cedric sharply. "We're giving two of them away."

"That's nice," said Mr Morgan, then drove off to tell his wife what generous, clever children they had.

"So what's the plan?" said Doris, when their father had gone.

"We're going to find the Naitabals and give them back the leaky raft," Cedric announced, "but only if they'll give us their tree-house for a week."

It took them a good twenty minutes to drag the three boats back to the river, launch them, and keep them under control until they were all safely on board *Naitabal II*. Then they untied the ropes and set off into the current with *Naitabal I* and the rowing boat in tow.

"I hope we don't meet that stranger again," said Cedric, glancing at the rowing boat.

They were well practised on the river by now, and their progress was reasonable. They entered the lake cautiously and circled Ghost Island, half expecting to see the Naitabals huddled together on the jetty, shivering and ready to offer any deal to be rescued and get their raft back again.

But the lake was empty, the house was just as blind and forbidding as before, and there was no sign of the Naitabals on the shores. They rowed to the far side of the lake, hoping to catch a glimpse of the Naitabals somewhere in the woods.

"What do we do now, clever dick?" said Doris, when they had reached the far end.

"We'll just leave the boats where we found them, shall we? Just take them to the jetty."

"That's not going to get us their tree-house, is it?"

"Well, have you got any bright suggestions?"

"No."

"Well, shut up, then."

Slowly, they began rowing back towards the jetty. When they reached it, they tied the rowing boat up, and were just about to release *Naitabal I* when they heard distant squeals of delight coming from the woods behind them.

"That was Charlotte!" said Cedric. "I bet that was Charlotte and the stupid old Naitabals!"

They immediately stopped untying *Naitabal I*, leaving it attached to their raft, and instinctively headed towards the shore with their listing booty in tow.

As the Naitabals swarmed round the horse chestnut tree, it seemed such an obvious hiding-place. They found its missing top was lying on the far side, where it must have fallen many years before, virtually rotted away, covered with the plants and fungi and lichen of a lot more than fourteen years.

Towering above them, the huge tree was almost bare of leaves by now, and their feet crunched and crackled in the browned remains of its fallen autumn cargo.

"I bet the treasure's in the fork between the two main branches," said Charlotte. "I can feel it in my bones."

"We've got to get up there, first," said Boff. "It doesn't look an easy climb."

Ben was already circling round the thick trunk, looking for footholds in the smooth bark when they heard a thin, eerie cry from the direction of the lake.

"Ahoy, Naitabals!"

The voice was weak and indistinct, carried on the light westerly breeze, but distinct enough for them to recognise not only the words 'Ahoy Naitabals', but the fact that it was Cedric Morgan's voice.

"Ahoy, Naitabals!"

The words came again, louder this time, and shriller.

"That was Doris Morgan, that time," said Jayne.

"Ahoy, Naitabals!" A chorus of all four voices.

Charlotte looked cross.

"Typical!" she said. "Just when we're about to do the most exciting part of the mystery, the Igmopong have to come interfering. Come on, Jayne, we'll go down and sort them out and get our raft back!"

The two of them set off down the hill, red-faced and full of purpose. When they arrived at the edge of the lake, they were greeted by the sight of the Igmopong about fifteen metres from the shore on *Naitabal II*, with *Naitabal I* empty and on tow, listing in the water.

"So you've brought our raft back, have you?" said Charlotte. "Why did you bother to call us? Just leave it here and go home before you catch cold or – preferably – drown or something."

"We want something for it," said Cedric.

"You stole it," said Jayne. "Both of them. If you don't give them back, you'll be sorry."

"Oh, yeah?" said Doris. "What'll we be sorry about?"

"You'll see," said Jayne. "You're too scared to come ashore and find out, aren't you?"

"We don't want to come ashore," said Amanda. "We like being on the raft."

"Yeah," said Andy.

"Give us your tree-house for a week," said Cedric, generously, "and we'll give you back your raft. Otherwise, how are you going to get home?"

"Mind your own business," retorted Jayne. "When you're stuck with a brain like yours, the shape and size of a walnut, it's difficult to work it out, isn't it?"

"What about yours, then?" shouted Doris. "Yours is the size and shape of a . . . a . . . "

"Raft," said Andy.

"I'd laugh if you weren't so pathetic," said Charlotte. She grabbed Jayne's arm. "Come on, Jayne, they're wasting our time. Let's go."

The two Naitabals turned their backs on the Igmopong and marched up the slope and back into the woods. They ignored the taunts from the raft, resisting the temptation to sink to the level of their enemies.

"Well, Cedric, that worked a real treat, didn't it!" Doris spat the words at him as Jayne and Charlotte disappeared. "You said you were going to get a week in their tree-house in exchange for the raft?"

"They didn't seem to want it, did they?" said Cedric, disheartened.

"So what do we do now? Take it away again?"

Cedric looked beaten for a few more moments, but then a slow smile spread across his features.

"No," he said, laughing. "We'll leave it here for them."

"Oh, we will, will we? And what's so amusingly funny about that idea?"

"We'll leave it here for them," said Cedric, "but we'll turn it into a little surprise."

"What do you mean?"

"Yeah," said Andy. "What d'you mean?"

"Tell us," said Amanda.

Cedric, enjoying one of his rare moments of triumph, ordered them to tow *Naitabal I* to the shore. Meekly, they obeyed, dying to learn the wonderful idea that was brewing in his head. As soon as it was beached, he ordered them to drag it on to dry land. It was heavier than when they had lifted it the last time, because the leaking drum was nearly three-quarters full of water.

As the others watched, Cedric took his penknife from his pocket and started cutting neat holes in the other eleven drums.

Cedric couldn't stop sniggering by this time, and the others joined in.

"We'll cut the holes just above the water-line on the inside where they can't see them," he said. "Then, when they climb in, the holes will be *under* the water, and when they're halfway home, they'll sink!"

"Yes!" said Doris.

"Yes!" said Amanda.

"Yeah!" said Andy.

It took much longer than they thought, and they took it in turns to keep a lookout for returning Naitabals, and to shield what the others were doing from prying eyes.

At last the evil task was finished. Doris had even had the sense to punch small holes in the top of each drum to let the air out when the water came in at the bottom. They refloated the raft, put some heavy stones on its tow rope on the shore so that it couldn't drift away, then paddled away from the scene of the crime in *Naitabal II*.

"Let's watch," said Doris. "We can hide behind one of those other little islands across the lake."

"Good idea," said Cedric.

Silently, the Igmopong set out across the smooth water.

Jayne and Charlotte arrived back at the horse chestnut tree to find that Ben had succeeded in climbing to the fork in the trunk. He was standing, waiting for their return before investigating any further.

"The trunk's hollow," Ben explained. Then he bent down and started excavating leaves and earth from the hiding place that he had found in the trunk.

"We reckon the tree was wrecked about thirty years ago," said Boff. "The trunk's been rotting inside ever since. If Reg Masters did hide anything in there, it wouldn't have been found by metal detectors, not unless they lifted them up to the trees. It seems a bit unlikely."

Leaves and dirt and debris continued to rain down from Ben's efforts, and after several minutes there was a loud exclamation.

"It's here! I've found it!"

"What?"

"What have you found?"

"What is it, Ben?" Jayne could hardly contain herself. "Do you need any help?"

"It's a wooden box," came Ben's muffled voice from inside the trunk. "It's too heavy for me to move it. We'll need a rope."

Toby immediately ran off in the direction of Miss Smithers' house.

"I'll get one!" he called, and was gone.

A few minutes later, he was back with four or five metres of thick nylon cord. Ben had made no further progress. Charlotte was up the tree with him, and they were trying to clear enough space round the box to get a rope under it. Toby tossed the rope up to them.

"Miss Smithers wasn't there," he said, "but I found this in her outbuildings."

Another few minutes were spent while Ben and Charlotte tried to thread the rope round the box in such a way that they could both get a good hold for hauling it up. It took a lot longer than they had imagined, and became more frustrating for Jayne, Boff and Toby who had to wait below, unable to help.

At last, after half an hour, the box was dragged out.

"You won't believe this!" called Charlotte.

"What won't we believe?" said Jayne.

"The key's still in the lock!"

"I don't believe it!"

"Told you you wouldn't! But it is!"

"Don't open it until we can all see!"

The box was so heavy that it had to be re-tied on the rope so that they could lower it safely to the ground, using a branch as a pulley.

At last the moment had arrived. At last they would see what Reg Masters had hidden there fourteen years before.

They drew sticks to see who would have the privilege of opening the box, and Jayne won by drawing the shortest. The five of them crowded in close as Jayne turned the key and started to ease open the lid.

## CHAPTER SIXTEEN

# *The Stranger*

The Naitabals' eyes shone with excitement as Jayne's slim hands caressed the sides of the lid, and slowly lifted it up. Inside the heavy box they saw dozens of small brown hessian bags tightly packed together. Resting on top of the bags was a white sealed envelope.

"I opened the box," said Jayne. "Your turn, Charlotte. You can lift the first bag of gold. Here, Ben, you can open the envelope."

"There's enough for everyone," said Charlotte. "We'll *all* take out a bag of gold."

"Yes," said Toby, "but you go first."

No one said anything as Charlotte reached in and prised one of the bags from its resting-place. She felt its lovely heaviness and they all heard the click and rattle of its contents as she turned it upright and sat it on the other bags. With shaking fingers she loosened the pull-string and stretched open the top. Everyone had their tongues almost hanging out, waiting to see the shining gold sovereigns inside.

As soon as they saw what was concealed there, the silence stretched into a silence of shock. They were stunned. They gazed at the contents of the bag. Instead of the shining gold coins they had expected, their eyes settled on stone pebbles, different coloured pebbles, scores of them, staring blindly up at them, mocking them with their dull, worthless silence.

Boff spoke first.

"Someone's already been here." He said it quietly, knowing he was stating the obvious.

"I can't believe it!" said Jayne. "After all that work, solving all those clues, and puzzles . . ."

With sadness in their hearts, they checked more bags at random, but the story was the same. They could tell by the sound of the others that all fifty contained the same thing – worthless pebbles

Ben sighed and fingered the sealed envelope.

"Shall I bother to open this?" he said.

The others nodded, still numb with disappointment, but Toby brightened.

"Perhaps it's another clue," he said. It seemed their only spark of hope.

Ben tore open the white envelope and extracted the single folded sheet inside. He laid it flat and read the message on it, but was too upset to read it aloud. Instead, it was passed from hand to hand, from hand to eye, from eye to brain, until they had all read and understood the three simple words that were written on it in black ink:

RECEIVED, WITH THANKS

There was no date, no signature. Just three polite words and a comma. As if in a dream, still huddled tightly round the box, the Naitabals carefully replaced the bags again, laying them to rest. They felt as if they were at a funeral, burying dreams. Ben laid the note ceremoniously on top, and Jayne closed the lid and turned the key. She removed the key and slipped it into her jeans pocket. No one said anything.

Boff and Toby climbed the horse chestnut tree this time. In silence, they burrowed deep into the hollow trunk, checking to see if there might be another box buried there. They tossed out a little more soil and leaves, but soon came to the dead end of rotting wood in the hollow.

It was while this was happening that they first heard the

rhythmical snapping of twigs in the distance behind them. They all swung round and saw a man approaching. He had a shock of untidy dark hair, bushy eyebrows and a full beard and moustache. He was wearing a bright red tartan lumberjack's shirt and black jeans, and he spoke with a Scottish accent. He wasn't smiling.

"So," he said. "What have we here?"

"What's it to you?" said Ben, who was nearest the box.

"Och, it's everything to me," said the stranger. "I've been looking for that wee box for nigh on fourteen years."

Jayne fingered the key in her pocket.

"Who are you?" she said.

"Just a friend o' the box."

"Is it yours, then?" she said.

The man stared at her a moment.

"It doesn'ae belong to anyone else," he said.

"No, but is it yours?"

"Yes."

"Can you prove it?" said Boff from the tree.

"I don't think I have to prove anything to you, young man. If ya've any sense, ya'll just let me take it."

There was a long silence.

Jayne turned to the others and switched to Naitabal language.

"*All-shong e-wung et-ling im-heng ave-heng it-ing? E-thong ey-king is-ing in-ing y-ming ocket-pong.*"

The others nodded.

"You'd better take it, then," Jayne said, turning to the man again.

The stranger's beard twitched into a smile.

"What very sensible children," he said.

As he took a few steps nearer to the box, Ben, Jayne and Charlotte retreated to the base of the horse chestnut tree. They stood there in a group, two up the tree and three on the ground, looking like a group photograph.

The stranger stooped down and teased the lid of the box with his fingertips, tested its enormous weight, and joggled its muffled contents.

"Where's the key?" he said.

"There wasn't a key," Jayne lied, even as her fingertips caressed its outline in her pocket. "If there'd been a key, we'd have opened it."

"That's why we were still looking in the tree," Toby lied. "Hoping to find it. We thought it might have fallen out."

The stranger shrugged.

"It's no matter," he said. "I'll no need a key to open this."

With that, he tried to lift the box, but immediately realised how heavy it really was. He made a bigger effort, bent his knees, straightened his back, heaved it up to waist level, and started staggering down the hill. He had only gone a few paces when he stumbled and dropped it with a crash into the spongy undergrowth.

"Throw me that rope," he said.

Charlotte wanted to ask him if he ever said 'please', but the look he gave as she hesitated was so malevolent, she thought better of it. She wondered if he was the Bad Man of Peter's letter, and not to be trifled with. She bent down and retrieved the blue nylon rope near her feet, coiled it, and threw it towards the stranger.

There were no thanks, either. He tied one end of the rope round the box, three ways like a Christmas present. Then, holding the other end over his shoulder, he began hauling it down the slope towards the shore of the lake. Sometimes the box snagged on ridges or saplings or knots of bramble, but the man persevered and slipped gradually out of sight with his booty.

"Let's follow him," said Ben.

Boff and Toby climbed down the tree.

"He's going to get a big shock when he gets the box open, isn't he?" said Toby. "When he finds someone's beaten him to it."

"Come on," said Ben. "If we don't follow him now, we'll lose him."

"I don't think he'll shake us off that easily," said Jayne. "Not while he's dragging that big box of pebbles, anyway."

They began to see the irony then, and started laughing.

"I'd love to see his face when he opens it," said Charlotte. "Serve him right for being so rude."

At last the disappointment was wearing off, and the Naitabals scurried down the hill towards the lake.

The stranger, robbed of his rowing boat by the Igmopong, had been forced to bring his car all the way to the lake. Looking at the map, the only place he could reach, and still leave it out of sight of the children and the house, was a rough track at the far end of the lake. It had seemed a good idea at the time. It was less likely to be seen, and he could spy on the children without rousing any suspicion.

Everything had gone perfectly. He'd watched them for the entire morning, measuring and pacing and banging in sticks, and it was with some satisfaction that he'd seen them climbing a horse chestnut tree of all things and finding what he'd been hoping to find for the past fourteen years. He had to admit that they were clever kids.

They had also shown great sense in not trying to stop him taking the box. It was much better this way. They had had the satisfaction of finding it, and he would have the satisfaction of opening it and spending the contents after fourteen years of frustration.

But now he was regretting parking the car at the far end of the lake. The box was becoming heavier and more awkward by the minute, and his fifty-five-year-old back was beginning to twinge.

But as he emerged from the trees at the margin of the lake, he realised with a surge of joy that there was an easier and quicker way to get the box back to his car. It was sitting there in front of him like a gift from heaven – the kids' raft. It was waiting for him right there, tethered to the shore with a pile of rocks, inviting him on board.

By the time the Naitabals reached the edge of the trees, they had their next surprise. The Igmopong had apparently relented and left the raft for them, anchored to the shore. It was a strangely generous gesture from the Igmopong, and one that the Naitabals found difficult to comprehend.

Not that it made any difference. The stranger, too, had discovered it, commandeered it, and had just finished loading his precious box on to one of the front seats.

"So you're taking our raft as well, are you?" Boff shouted.

The stranger said nothing, didn't even look up at them. He manoeuvred the raft into position, kicked away the stones that were holding it to the shore, and walked it out into the lake until the water was deep enough for him to sit on the other front seat and start paddling.

"It's listing a bit," said Toby. "That leaky drum must be full of water by now."

They watched the raft as it made its way across the lake. As it neared the middle they began to sense that something was seriously wrong. The stranger must have realised it, too. He was paddling harder and harder to try to keep the raft moving, and the reason was becoming all too obvious. The raft was gradually getting lower and lower in the water.

The stranger's pathetic cry echoed across the lake.

"No-o-o-o-o-o!"

At that moment, the Naitabals turned to see *Naitabal II* coming on to the scene as if from nowhere. It was being frantically paddled by the Igmopong, but instead of turning to rescue the sinking man, his cries had made them paddle more frantically away from the scene of distress, and towards the jetty instead.

The Naitabals watched with a growing sense of satisfaction. The stranger's efforts to get anywhere near the shore grew more and more frantic and hopeless. Even the Igmopong stopped paddling and watched as the raft finally disappeared below the waterline. The stranger's stricken cry hit their ears again as he sank gracefully out of sight. All that could be seen at the end was a pool of bubbles and turbulence, and the stranger's head bobbing near the surface of the water.

There was a spontaneous cheer from the Naitabals. Then Ben spoke slowly.

"That was meant for us. *That* was why the Igmopong were being so kind, leaving the raft for us."

The Naitabals' laughter died away. The enemy had got all he deserved, but the situation was still serious. He had now started swimming steadily towards the jetty where his rowing boat was moored.

Behind their screen of long grass on the little island, the Igmopong had been sitting on board *Naitabal II*, waiting patiently to see the wonderful sight of the Naitabals climbing aboard their raft, paddling out into the lake, and sinking. They could hardly contain their excitement.

When at last they saw a movement at the edge of the trees, it wasn't one of the Naitabals, but someone dragging a heavy box on the end of a piece of rope.

"It's that man!" squeaked Doris. "It's that man we took the rowing boat from!"

They watched in horror as he stopped at the raft and started manhandling his box on to it. They realised exactly what would happen. They didn't know how long it would take to sink, but they'd made quite big holes in the drums, and they didn't suppose it would stay afloat very long once there was some weight on it.

"That stupid man's taking the raft!" Doris exploded

suddenly. "He's going to spoil our fun!"

"I was looking forward to watching the stupid Naitabals sink," said Amanda.

"And get soaking wet," said Andy.

Cedric, in an unusual bout of clear-thinking, was way ahead of Doris already.

"We'd better start moving – quick," he said. "We'll be in trouble if we don't."

"Why?" snapped Doris. "It's that bloke who's going to sink, not us."

"Yes," said Cedric impatiently. "And when the raft sinks, he's going to swim, isn't he? He's probably seen his rowing boat already, tied to the jetty. And he's going to swim to it, isn't he? And when he swims to it, he's going to get in it. And when he's in it, he's going to see us and row in our direction and do something nasty because we pinched his boat."

"He might hit us," said Amanda.

"Or murder us," said Andy.

"Or *sink* us," said Cedric, with feeling.

By this time, the stranger had already set off from the shore with his cargo. It was obvious straight away that he was heading for the far end of the lake rather than his rowing boat.

"Come on," hissed Cedric. "Let's get the rowing boat before he does. Let's go!"

With a lot of splashing and frantic paddling, the Igmopong emerged from the cover of the little grassy island and set off in the direction of the jetty. The stranger saw them at the same moment as the Naitabals appeared on the shore. By the time the stranger was nearly halfway up the lake, it was clear to him and everyone watching that he and his raft were heading for only one place – the bottom of the lake.

As it started sinking, the Igmopong stopped rowing for a moment and held their breath. In the eerie silence that followed they watched open-mouthed as the raft, the box and the stranger slowly descended into the dark depths of the unknown. From the stranger's lips had come a strangled cry of pain and despair, a long drawn-out "No-o-o-o-o-o!", followed by a huge cheer from the distant Naitabals.

The Igmopong saw the stranger starting to swim in the direction of the jetty, just as Cedric had predicted. They doubled their efforts and reached the rowing boat in plenty of time to miss the stranger's arrival. They untied it, and while Andy held the painter, they towed it towards the Naitabals on the shore.

The Naitabals watched the Igmopong coming closer and closer, and for yet another silly moment believed that their enemies were bringing a boat for them out of the kindness of their hearts. But when the Igmopong were still twenty metres off shore, Cedric gave the command to stop.

The stranger was way behind them, still swimming towards the jetty, so Cedric calculated that they had plenty of time to negotiate before fate caught up with them. He turned to the Naitabals.

"We'll give you a boat if you'll give us a week in your tree-house!" he called.

The Igmopong, however, in their final hour of greed and treachery, had miscalculated.

Ben had been measuring the distance between the shore and the boats, and even before any of the Naitabals had bothered to reply to Cedric's ludicrous demand, Ben had run forward and dived headlong into the dark water of the lake. The sudden coldness of it hit him like an arctic wind, chilling him through to the bone, it seemed. He gasped to the surface and struck out in quick strokes towards the Igmopong.

The Igmopong panicked. They tried to get under way, but before they had time to get their oars in the water and make a few strokes, Ben had reached them. He grabbed Cedric and clung on to him like an octopus, hauling him down towards the water.

"Got you!" shouted Ben. "Now row to the shore!"

Cedric, frightened of being half-drowned, yelled out in a pathetic bleat.

"*Help*! *Doris*! *Do what he says*!"

"Don't!" shouted Doris to the others. "*Don't* do what he says. Cedric's just being a baby! Let's just row away!"

Quick as lightning, Ben dunked Cedric's head several times to make him splutter, then released him and grabbed Doris. As he tried to pull her out of the raft, her screams rang out across the lake and came echoing back to them. They were louder than Cedric's, but her words were exactly the same.

"*Help*! *Cedric*! *Do what he says*!"

"Come on," said Cedric. He glared at his stricken sister. She was hanging sideways from the raft, her legs trapped in the middle, with Ben dragging her top half down towards the water. "Do what the big baby says."

The raft was brought to shore with Andy still holding the rowing boat. "If you don't get out of our raft *now*," said Ben, releasing Doris, "we'll tip you out."

The Igmopong got out.

Ben took the oars away from the rowing boat and stowed them on the raft.

"Now get in the rowing boat," he ordered.

The Igmopong got in.

"And don't try any fancy tricks, or we'll tip you out of that, as well."

The stranger had made it to the jetty by now, and was lying flat out, exhausted, in a pool of water, recovering his breath.

The Naitabals boarded *Naitabal II* and took control of it while the Igmopong sat helplessly in the oarless boat. The Naitabals had a brief huddled whisper together. Then, holding the rowing boat in tow, they paddled out towards the jetty. Their plan was to circumnavigate it and head for the river entrance, but they wanted some reaction from the Igmopong first.

"We don't want to go to the jetty," said Cedric, panicking.

"Why not?" said Charlotte, all innocence.

Cedric leaned towards the Naitabals in a whisper.

"Because we're in that man's boat. We took it!"

"We'll give it back to him, then," said Charlotte, simply.

The jetty loomed nearer and nearer.

"But we can't get nine people on your raft," said Cedric.

"No, and we're not going to try," said Charlotte.

"But if he takes his boat back, we won't have a boat. We won't be able to get home . . ."

Charlotte turned to look at the Igmopong's faces.

"Oh dear," she said, heartlessly.

They were within fifty metres of the jetty now, but the Naitabals weren't going to make the same mistake the Igmopong had made. They started to curve outwards in an arc, keeping Ghost Island at a safe distance. The stranger had recovered his breath and was climbing to his feet.

At the same moment, Boff suddenly spotted something floating in the water. He reached out and scooped it up, held it in his hand and looked at it. It was a small patch of dark hair, about four centimetres long.

"That's far enough," said Boff, and everyone stopped paddling. He showed his find to the others, who looked mystified. Then he called across the water to the stranger.

"We were so sorry to see your boat sink," he said. "Now we'll never know what was in the box."

They could see the stranger's face, even at that distance, clouded with anger. It looked lopsided somehow. He pointed a shaking finger at them.

"That's my boat, there!" he said, accusingly. "They stole it! I want it back, and I want it back now before I freeze to death."

"You can have it back," said Boff, calmly. "If you tell us who you are, and why you followed us, and how you knew about the hidden box."

"I'm no telling you anything."

"I think you might," said Boff, clutching the tuft of hair tightly in his hand. "Because if you don't, we think the police would like to hear what you've been doing today."

"You stole my boat," said the stranger. "That's the only thing the police would be interested in. And the box is at the bottom of the lake. What's that got to do with me?"

"There are nine people here who saw you take it to the bottom of the lake," said Boff. "I think the police would like to know exactly where it is so they can send some frogmen down to have a look at it."

"Just give me my boat back and stop interfering with grown-up things you don't understand," snapped the stranger. "You've had your fun finding the wee box, and now it's gone. Let's all go home."

"So that you can come back one night with diving gear and fetch it up again?" said Boff.

The stranger started to become impatient.

"What's all this to do with you, anyway?" he said. "Why don't you just shove off and leave it alone? Before you get hurt."

"We're not leaving until you've told us the story," said Boff. "Because we're very curious about it. We went to a lot of trouble to find that box, and we want to know how you came to be involved. Otherwise, we'll tell the police."

"I'm not telling you anything."

Boff stared hard across the fifty metres of water as their raft gently rocked in the wavelets.

"I think you are," he said. "We know your address. We know what job you used to have, and why you lost it. And we know your name."

"Don't talk nonsense."

"And all because of this," said Boff, holding up the little tuft of hair in his hand.

"I can't see what you're holding from here, stupid."

"No," said Boff, "but you can *feel* what I'm holding from there."

"Stop talking in riddles."

"Feel your *face*," shouted Boff.

The other Naitabals stared at him as his words carried to the jetty.

"Feel your *eyebrows!*" Boff continued. He held the tuft higher in the air. "I think you'll find there's one missing!"

The stranger put a hand up to his face and felt across his forehead as Boff's voice cut across the water.

"There *is* one missing, isn't there? *Mr Jarmyn!*"

## CHAPTER SEVENTEEN

# *Received, With Thanks*

No words of denial came across the water from the stranger. Instead, in a sudden burst of temper, he tore off his remaining eyebrow and beard and wig and hurled them into the water in disgust.

There were gasps of surprise from the other Naitabals.

"We can go to the jetty now," said Boff, calmly. "We know who we're dealing with – thank goodness it isn't the Bad Man that Peter warned us about."

The Naitabals pulled strongly on their paddles, and as soon as the front of the raft touched the jetty, Ben stepped off to tie it up. Boff joined him and stood facing the 'stranger' – Mr Jarmyn, clean-shaven, with thin, silvery hair – calm now and shivering on the jetty.

"You stole my code!" was the first thing Mr Jarmyn had to say. Not only had all the false hair gone, but the Scottish accent had been stripped as well, exposing his very ordinary English tones.

"We did *solve* your code, Mr Jarmyn," Boff said, being careful not to put their friend Peter at risk, "but what it told us looked like something criminal. That's why we didn't tell you."

"No. But you went to find it yourself, instead?"

"Only out of curiosity," said Boff. "We don't care what happens to it now. Perhaps if you tell us your story, we might not bother going to the police."

"You sound as if you know it already," said Mr Jarmyn.

"You knew Reg Masters, didn't you?" Boff began. "The man who wrote the code? You knew Reg Masters," Boff continued, staring at him, "*because you were the police officer investigating the case*."

There was a second gasp from the other Naitabals as Mr Jarmyn stared back hard at Boff.

"How could you possibly know that . . .?"

"It was you who arrested him, and it was you who locked him up – wasn't it? He was in one of your cells when he died, wasn't he? I don't think he had a copy of the code with him in the police cell, but I think you must have found it when you searched Ghost Island."

"How can you possibly know this?" said Mr Jarmyn, shocked. "You're just a child. How can you know this?"

"We've spoken to Miss Smithers," said Boff, evading the truth about Peter, keeping him safely out of it. "She has problems with her memory, but she told us that the man in charge of the case reminded her of Cinderella – it only occurred to me when I found your eyebrow in the water – not a glass slipper, just an eyebrow. You remind her of Cinderella because your name is like Prince Charming – that's how she remembered it – Prince Jarmyn!"

Mr Jarmyn stared and said nothing more.

"What I can't understand," said Boff, "is why Reg Masters would have kept a copy of the code at all? He knew where he'd hidden the haul, so why keep a copy of the code that was meant for his accomplice?"

Mr Jarmyn still stared.

"You weren't his accomplice, were you?" said Boff.

"Don't be ridiculous!" said Mr Jarmyn, stung into speech at last. "He wrote the code out for his accomplice all right – not that we'll ever know who his accomplice was – and no, he didn't keep a copy. He'd written the code on a pad of paper and torn off the top sheet to send it in the post. The copy I found was an impression on the sheet of paper underneath. He'd overlooked that. You can often read the previous letter that someone's written by looking at the dents in the sheet on the top of the pad. But I was greedy. I didn't keep it for police evidence. It was a seemingly blank piece of paper, so I tore it off and slipped it into my pocket. If the case wasn't solved, I knew I could come looking for the stuff when I retired."

"Thank you. That's all we want to know. But don't come near any of us ever again. Don't come to our streets, or our village, or into our woods. If we see you, we'll call the police straight away and tell them what's at the bottom of this lake, and who was on the raft when it sank. I hope you understand?"

Mr Jarmyn stared at Boff, straight in his eyes. The Naitabals all stared at Mr Jarmyn.

Mr Jarmyn, cold and wet, knew when he was beaten.

"Is it all right if I . . . come here?" he said. He nodded his head towards the middle of the lake.

"As long as you don't come near us, we don't care what you do," said Boff.

The Igmopong had sat quietly in the rowing boat all this time, hoping that Mr Jarmyn still hadn't seen them. They didn't understand a word of what had been going on. They didn't understand how the Naitabals had disappeared off the jetty, and they didn't understand how Mr Jarmyn had disappeared off the jetty. They didn't understand what was on the raft when it sank, and they hadn't the faintest idea who the man was, or why Boff was telling him what he could do and what he couldn't do. They were only sure of one thing: the Naitabals wouldn't be enlightening *them*.

But now Boff had swung round and was pointing at them in the boat. He spoke to Mr Jarmyn again.

"Your boat, I believe?" he said.

Mr Jarmyn noticed the Igmopong again and glared at them.

"Yes," he said.

"You'd better have it back, then," said Boff. He handed Mr Jarmyn its tow rope and its oars. The Igmopong stared in horror as the Naitabals boarded *Naitabal II* and paddled slowly away.

As the Naitabals went, they watched the scene unfolding on the jetty. First, Mr Jarmyn asked the Igmopong to get out. The Igmopong refused. They tried to pull the rope from Mr Jarmyn's hand. Mr Jarmyn held firm and asked them again. The Igmopong refused. Mr Jarmyn told them if they weren't out in ten seconds, they would be in the water in eleven.

The Igmopong climbed out.

Mr Jarmyn thanked them courteously, said goodbye, and rowed back towards the far end of the lake where his car was parked.

The Naitabals, satisfied, propelled themselves towards the entrance to the river.

Cedric's pitiful voice wafted across the water from the jetty.

"You're not going to leave us here, are you?"

"We'll tell your parents where you are," said Charlotte. "They shouldn't be *too* long."

"We don't know how they'll get you off," Jayne joined in, "but they'll think of *something*."

Even in his distress, Cedric couldn't resist asking the one question that had been burning a hole in his brain.

"How did you disappear when we took your boat?" he called.

"Didn't you know?" Ben called back, calmly. "The house is haunted. It's not called Ghost Island for nothing. The ghost took us in through the wall."

The other Naitabals laughed, and the Igmopong sensed it was the only answer they would get. But it sent a creepy feeling up the backs of their necks, and they all turned to look at the blank wall of Ghost Island.

When Miss Smithers returned from shopping, she found a

tape measure and a ball of string on her doorstep and a Thank You note from the Naitabals. A big red light inside her back door was flashing and a little alarm was buzzing. She pressed the reset button to stop the noise.

"So there's someone on the lake, is there?" she said aloud to herself. "I hope it's those *nasty* children who stranded the N . . . what were they called? . . .and pinched their boat . . . If it is, I'll teach them a lesson . . ."

She made her way down the tunnel at impressive speed and arrived inside Ghost Island within a few minutes. She didn't turn on any house lights, but made her way by torchlight to one of the window slots that overlooked the western side of the lake, across the main expanse of water. Nothing. She moved to a north window, looked out through a peep-hole, and spotted a raft. It was travelling round the bend into the river entrance, carrying the five children who had stayed at the house. Finally, she looked on to the jetty, and was surprised to find a man in a rowing boat pulling away from it, leaving behind the four nasty children – the ones who had stolen the two boats and stranded everyone else.

She wasted no time. She opened a tin of white powder and powdered her face and hands, checking in the mirror until she had the pallor of a ghost. Then she put dark make-up in her eye sockets until she looked more like a skeleton. She took down the long white hooded robe that hung on a hook on the west wall, and quickly pulled it over her clothes. She pulled on waterproof overshoes, then made a final check of her victims through the spy-hole.

She pressed a big fat button on a control panel and stood back. A thundering, grating sound filled the air. A huge stone slab that blocked up the old west door rumbled sideways into a recess in the wall, and the evening sunlight flooded in through the opening that was revealed.

Outside, just beneath the surface of the water, another

stone slab slid out from the house to make a causeway between two of the posts. Miss Smithers composed herself, then stepped outside, moving gracefully on the causeway with her feet just touching the surface of the water. She was aware of screams and shouts and cries from the jetty, but walked on, acting her part. When she was five metres from the house she turned and slowly, majestically, walked back into the house through the open wall. The grinding, grating rub of stone on stone echoed round the house and the lake, and Miss Smithers, the ghost of Ghost Island, disappeared once again.

The Igmopong, sitting on the jetty in their life-jackets, with their bare feet dangling in the water, heard the grating sound behind them and turned to see what it was.

They all stared open-mouthed at the white hooded apparition that was standing on the surface of the water beyond the posts that surrounded the house. Even as they watched in horror, the figure raised its arms and gestured towards them as if it were casting a spell on them.

Amanda screamed, Doris went bright red, and Cedric and Andy's faces went as white as the plastic drums on *Naitabal II*.

"It's the g-g-g-ghost!" shrieked Doris.

As they watched, goggle-eyed and horror-struck, the figure turned slowly and disappeared into the wall of the house.

The Igmopong clung to each other in fear, and all screeched in one breath the only word that comes easily with a scream.

"*H-e-e-e-e-e-e-e-e-l-l-l-l-l-p!*"

"Do you realise," said Ben, when the Naitabals were back in the seclusion of the tree-house, and Cedric's parents had been given the bad news, "that if it hadn't been for the Igmopong, we'd never have found out anything?"

"How?" said Jayne.

"Well, if they hadn't stolen our raft, Toby wouldn't have fallen in the water, and if Toby hadn't fallen in the water, Miss Smithers wouldn't have taken pity on us and let us into Ghost Island."

"And if they hadn't brought the boats back . . ." said Jayne.

"And if they hadn't punctured the plastic drums . . ." said Toby.

Boff looked round at them all and allowed one of his rare smiles to break out on to the surface.

"Yes," he said, "but we're not going to tell the Igmopong that, are we?"

"Do we tell Peter what's happened?" said Jayne.

Boff considered.

"Yes," he said. Without further thought, he pulled a blank sheet of paper towards him and started writing. The others leaned over his shoulder to read.

*Dear 'Peter',*

*Code solved, but secret safe. No chance of discovery in a million years, but evidence sufficient to convict Bad Man if he ever makes trouble.*

*Your 'anonymous' friends.*

The others approved.

"It's better if he doesn't know," concluded Boff. "If we told him what it all meant, and that the gold has gone, he might lose his confidence fighting the Bad Man. It's best if they *both* think the secret is still a secret."

It was the following day when, recovered from their ordeal on the jetty, the Igmopong leaned over the fence into the Sea of Debris and spoke to Charlotte, who was cleaning the windows of the Naitabal hut.

"What was in that box that sank with the raft?" Cedric

asked, trying to sound casual.

"Gold," said Charlotte.

Two days later, the Igmopong were building a submarine.

It was (though no one knew it) the lifting and dragging and burying of the box in the horse chestnut tree that had eventually damaged Reg Masters' already weak heart, and caused his death the following night in police custody.

For an individual person, working on his own, to retrieve the same locked box, weighing thirty-five kilos, from the bottom of a lake, is a virtually impossible task.

Whether Mr Jarmyn ever attempted it, or succeeded, we will never know. Did he go down with an oxyacetylene torch and cut a hole in the lid so that the contents could be taken out in manageable chunks? Did he find a crooked friend he could trust (as far as one can trust a crooked friend) to help him up with it? We will never know that, either.

But what if he did? Suppose he managed to achieve the near-impossible? We will never know the look that might have come over his face as he opened the box and found fifty bags of pebbles inside, all tied neatly in little linen money pouches. Neither will we know the bad words – the very bad words – he might have spoken, or the terrible rage in his heart and his mind. It might have been enough to give *him* a heart attack, too.

But we *do* know that he wouldn't have been able to read the note that lay on top of the bags. The water would have dissolved the writing in a few short days: the words that once said, simply,

RECEIVED, WITH THANKS

## EPILOGUE

It is the last day of the month.

At five o'clock in the afternoon, Miss Smithers locks all her doors and draws all her curtains. She unrolls the carpet in her sitting-room, unscrews the floorboards, and exposes the hiding place of a wooden box. She opens the lid and moves aside the pieces of paper wrapped neatly in a rubber band. She gazes at the thousands of gold sovereigns lying underneath.

It is time for her to receive her regular monthly payment – the payment she has earned for keeping the house on Ghost Island clean and tidy – and free from unwelcome visitors.

She removes twenty-five gold coins and places them in her purse. In its proper place, within the rubber band, she adds another piece of paper.

She writes the day's date on it, and the words,

TWENTY-FIVE GOLD SOVEREIGNS
RECEIVED, WITH THANKS

She closes her eyes for a moment and remembers a late night almost fourteen years ago when she couldn't sleep. She remembers wandering into the fresh air of the woods, and hearing strange sounds a little way off. She remembers hiding and watching Reg Masters hauling a heavy box into a tree.

She says a prayer and opens her eyes. She closes the lid of the box and replaces the floorboards and the carpet. She opens her curtains and goes into the kitchen to make a cup of tea.

Did you enjoy *Ghost Island*?

If you would like to know how Peter's story leads to the events in *Ghost Island*, you can read it in David Schutte's

## SKELETONS IN THE ATTIC

ISBN 1-904028-04-7 £5.00

*Peter stared at Joe, unable to speak, his neck and jaw muscles paralysed and his eyes filling with tears. Joe, alarmed, picked up the diary from where it had fallen and frantically turned the pages. . .*

Peter, recovering from the sudden death of his mother six weeks before, has never known his father, believing him to be dead. His horrible Uncle Len has moved in, and Peter's future is looking bleak.

Then disturbing things start happening. First, a strange man in a sports car starts watching the house and asking the neighbours questions. Then someone telephones Peter, claiming to be his father. It's only when Peter and his friend Joe start messing around in the attic that they find something so shocking that it changes Peter's life for ever. . .

(There are no Naitabals in this book, but the story sets the scene for the fifth Naitabal mystery, *Ghost Island.)*

***"I enjoyed this book very much and would definitely recommend it to my friends."***

**Paul Bailey, aged 9**

***"Skeletons in the Attic is a brilliant book."***

**Chloe Jones, aged 10**

There are now six books in
David Schutte's Naitabal Mystery series.

If you enjoyed this book, you'll love the others!

## 1. DANGER, KEEP OUT!

ISBN 1-904028-00-4 £5.00

*Miss Coates steamed up the garden path. Her white hair glowed in the moonlight. She stopped at the well in the middle of her lawn, and shone her torch into it. And then . . . she disappeared.*

To ordinary people, she's Miss Coates, but to the Naitabals she's the old enemy battleship, the SS *Coates*. And she's hiding something. Why has she grown huge hedges around her garden, so no one can see into it? And why is she so desperate to stop anyone snooping?

Determined to discover the truth, the Naitabals go investigating. But the secrets they uncover lie deep in the past – a past that Miss Coates will do anything to conceal. . .

***"Get ready for an invasion of wild ten-year-olds... "***

**The Daily Telegraph**

## 2. WAKE UP, IT'S MIDNIGHT!

ISBN 1-904028-01-2 £5.00

*Charlotte stood, hand poised on the doorknob, and took a deep breath. The ghostly sound of typing stopped abruptly, as suddenly as it had begun. She threw open the door. A piece of paper in the old typewriter fluttered in the moving air. But there was no one there.*

The Mysterious Motionless Mr Maynard hasn't moved for two days. Beneath that hairless head and ferocious scowl, his evil brain is plotting – but plotting what?

A secret drawer, an empty house at midnight, a missing manuscript, spying, cheating – and a mysterious lady in black – are just a few of the obstacles the Naitabals must overcome to solve the mystery. Wake up, it's midnight! Join the Naitabals in their second breathtaking adventure!

***"The type of story that would appeal to juniors who like reading about children outwitting the adults. . . who dream of having a tree-house and outdoor adventures, and who like codes and secret letters. It is all very entertaining. . ."***

**Junior Bookshelf**

More Naitabal Mysteries by David Schutte

## 3. WILD WOODS, DARK SECRET

ISBN 1-904028-02-0 £5.00

*The woman was moving along a track a little way above them. Instead of walking, she seemed to be sailing effortlessly, floating like a ghost above the ground. . .*

The Naitabal gang are promised the holiday of a lifetime at Mr Blake's remote country house. But from the very first moment, their visit is plunged into mystery.

Why has Mr Blake disappeared? What is the meaning of the weird coded messages? Who are the sinister strangers that prowl the dark, forbidding woods?

Only one thing is clear – Mr Blake is in big trouble. . .

***"The Naitabals are a wild species of human aged about 10 who inhabit these great books. . . I hope David Schutte can keep adding to the series. . ."***

**The School Librarian**

## 4. BEHIND LOCKED DOORS

ISBN 1-904028-03-9 £5.00

*The message was written in purple ink on yellow paper. In an almost illegible spidery scrawl, it said...*
*'PLEASE HELP ME!'*

Mrs Hooper has not left her home or spoken to anyone for twenty years, ever since her husband died. His hat, coat and umbrella still hang in the hall, untouched, covered in dust.

Now the Naitabals realise she might be in trouble. What sinister secrets are hidden within Mrs Hooper's spooky old house? Why has she locked herself away for so long? When the Naitabals finally open the locked doors, they find a mystery far more evil than any of them could have imagined . . .

***"Have you got a Naitabal in your garden? According to author David Schutte, a Naitabal is 'a wild species of human aged about ten', it feeds on 'anything, except what its parents want it to' and it lives mainly in tree-houses. If your own Naitabal hankers for . . . adventure, buy it one of Schutte's Naitabal Mysteries."***

**The Times**

Another Naitabal Mystery by David Schutte. . .

## 6. DEAD MAN'S CHEST

ISBN 1-904028-06-3 £5.00

*It was a light oak box strengthened with metal straps like a pirate's treasure chest. The edges of the lid were decorated with silhouettes of pirate figures burnt into the wood. Charlotte read the message branded on the lid across the middle: 'SARAH'S LITTLE TREASURE'.*

The Naitabals have never seen a living soul at the lonely Deep Shadow Cottage in Gray's Wood. But when Jayne catches a glimpse of a face at the window, it heralds a chain of events that plunge even the woods themselves into danger.

Who really owns the cottage? How did a burning house link its tenant with a past cloaked in mystery?

The fifteen pirates burnt into the lid of the dead man's little wooden chest are just one of the clues that lead the Naitabals to the stunning secret.

and David Schutte's tale of adventure in Cumbria. . .

## SAM AND THE U.F.O.

ISBN 1-904028-07-1 £5.00

*It came from the south-west, and it was glowing with a brilliant pink light. At first Sam thought it must be an aeroplane. But it was coming lower and lower, bending slowly towards the earth.*

The arrangement had been simple, and safe: Sam's parents would see him on to the train in London, and Sam's uncle would meet him at the station in Carlisle. But when Sam rings home to say that he has arrived safely, he isn't telling the whole truth. He has known all along that his uncle won't be there. He takes a taxi to his uncle's lonely cottage and finds it locked and silent.

When Uncle Black finally turns up, he is badly shocked to see Sam. Why is he so hot-tempered? What is hidden in the locked room in the cottage?

Sam begins a battle of wits with his uncle, and the discovery of the tiny UFO and its occupants leads Sam and two new friends into an adventure that they – and the world – will never forget.

***"An original, fast-moving and thoroughly entertaining book. More than enough suspense and humour to keep the reader entertained to the end."***

**Lance Salway**

Junior Genius